RAGEBORN

BATTLEBORN TRILOGY BOOK 2

PAUL SATING

PAUL SATING

Editor: Cindy Niespodzianski

Cover Design: Cover art © Vivid Covers | www.VividCovers.com

ISBN-13: 979-8-9857203-1-0

FREE PAUL SATING FANTASY

To Erica Stensrud. Everyone should have a friend and cheerleader like you in their lives! Thank you for every single one of your kind acts.

haven
lake

havennun

shadowfell

valley of the
river song

white plains

dead queen forest

dunkel
cove

the river song

zena's crowns

hastelle
dam

wood forest

evelence

shallow
sea

fortune
falls

elle

shelding
booms

shadar

GREEN SEA

1

GAERON

GAERON SLASHED as he rolled underneath the giant scorpion.

It reared, screeching. Somehow, its rider remained saddled, keeping control of the beast that thrust its thirty-foot long tail at Gaeron. The ground shook each time the thick appendage pierced it. Importantly, the beast missed, leaving Gaeron alive to shout at his friend.

"Stab the damn thing!"

Behind the tail, Drulf Bural stabbed and slashed. His sword deflected off the beast's tough carapace as if the paladin was using a training stick.

Chali Danos, the most powerful Chaos Bender in Olma-Ka, had little to work with. Her magic depended on the environment. She could only draw on nearby elements. Being west of the Sweet Waters River, she could only pull from the endless sand. With Gaeron and Drulf near the beast, she couldn't devour the scorpion in a sandstorm or even a vortex, which forced her to target in her spells more accurately. So far, they were useless, and Gaeron doubted they could count on her unless he and Drulf could make a coordinated dash away from the scorpion, leaving enough space for her to attack. The way the fight was going, that wasn't likely.

If they made it back to Olma-Ka, he promised himself to get her on the training fields with a staff in her hand. At least a bow, though he wasn't sure she could use arrows since Benders had a strange affliction to edged weapons. Magic— too often useless.

The massive tail, broader than any boar back in Olma-Ka, thrust and he rolled. That attack was the closest yet.

The scorpion rider was a ranger. Whenever the scorpion allowed him the stability to load and fire his bow, he did, targeting Drulf more often than the Chaos Bender. The big Buk Toh, the Olmarian term for the pale people of walled cities, was the more immediate threat in the rider's eyes, which was fine with Gaeron. They needed Chali to attack, and soon. As long as she wasn't the one being attacked, she could concoct something to bring a victory. They harassed the beast so constantly and chaotically that it thrashed and spun, denying the rider more than a couple of shots, none of them clear.

"If you run, I have a spell that will end this," Chali shouted over the screeching.

"I don't run," Gaeron barked.

"Then you keep fighting," Chali said.

Gaeron growled. Not that long ago, he'd fought another scorpion rider. A large squad of riders had attacked an Olmarian squad, twice their size but exhausted from a long and treacherous journey from the city of Hastelle across the desert. Half the Olmarians died that day. No one came out unscathed but Gaeron's brother, Nevilan. While the few survivors came away with injuries, in body and mind, he came out with his second Mark, the Olmarian symbol of freedom and status. The Paramount had carved it into his forehead the night of their return. Nevilan celebrated as if the journey had been the greatest success in Olmarian history, even while the village mourned their dead.

Gaeron didn't plan for any of them to suffer at the hands

of this rider, though. This journey was supposed to be a relatively simple mission into the Dark Sands meant to get him away from his older brother. At least until the leader of Olma-Ka could figure out what to do with the pair. Maybe it was naïve of them, but they hadn't planned on sneak attacks from Scorpion Riders.

Gaeron shouted to draw the rider's attention, lunging toward the scorpion. His sword shuddered against the beast, skipping off as if he'd struck rock. His hands tingled with vibrations. "You tough bastard," he said, shaking off the sensation.

"Move now!" the Chaos Bender shouted.

Both men complied. Drulf dove over a small mound of sand, sheering off the top. Gaeron swung his blade, connecting with the outside of the scorpion's pincer and spinning it in the opposite direction, before joining his friend.

Chali held a large ball of rotating sand above her, twice the size of the scorpion's head. The ball dwarfed the Bender. As soon as Gaeron and Drulf were clear, she blasted it at the creature and rider. The scorpion screeched; the rider yelled in a foreign tongue. The chains of gold weaving in and out of his thighs jingled. The human covered his eyes with his forearm, holding onto the reins with a single hand. The beast was too dumb and spun aimlessly.

The face full of sand confused it. Gaeron sensed nervousness from the rider and unsettled mount.

He raced forward, lowering his shortsword, diving and rolling underneath the beast's chelicera just as it snapped at him with a pedipalp. A loud *clack* told him the pincer had been close. Too close. With the giant above him and the dust from Chali's dissipating spell settling to the ground and tickling his nose, he stared up at the golden skin covered in long, brown hair. The pods of its thorax were out of reach. Its foremost claws snapped as they blindly reached to snag this new threat. Gaeron had a moment, nothing more, before the rider adjusted his arachnid mount and left Gaeron exposed and on his back.

He thrust his sword into the softer skin between its front and second set of legs. The blade bit deep. The surge of violence filled him, his chest burning with the desire to feel the heat of the beast's blood. Bloodlust born. He pushed as the arachnid screeched above him. His sword sank to the cross-guard. Black ichor spilled from the wound. Gaeron pulled his sword down even as the beast's life source covered him. He ripped and tore as his chest and arms were painted black in its death, ripping open the mount.

The giant scorpion reared, trying to pull free. When it did, Gaeron rolled out from underneath, and was on his feet before it settled back to the soft sand. He pushed against it as it reared. He howled as he called on his reserves and sprinted at the exposed underbelly. Jamming his sword into it again, Gaeron didn't wait for it to lash out or recover. Placing his hands on its skin, heated by blood and battle, he pushed. The raw strength, emboldened by his bloodlust, powered his back, his shoulders, his arms. He thrust.

The giant beast toppled onto its back, crushing the human rider.

The dying creature's eight claws swatted at the air as it tried to regain its footing. With a shake of his head, Gaeron climbed atop it and pulled his sword free. Raising the weapon, he plunged it into the wiggling scorpion and sliced open the length of its body. Innards sprayed from its cavity, some striking his face before falling to the desert floor.

He stood atop the dead scorpion, covered in its stinking blood and heaving deep breaths.

From below, Chali grinned, a playful twinkle in her eyes. "Well, I can't say you haven't looked better."

Gaeron snorted and jumped to the sand, scooping a handful and using it to clean as much of the black blood as he could. "We need to find water. This stinks."

"That's your normal smell," Drulf said, huffing as if he'd been the one to topple the beast.

Chali jerked her head at the corpse. A single human arm, tattooed with their culture's ceremonial sigils, protruded from underneath the scorpion. "Nice work tipping that over on him. Though, now I'm not sure how we're going to check for valuables, you big oaf."

"For every savage who dies, no Olmarian mother cries," Gaeron cited the old Olmarian saying, teasing her even though he only now realized she was right.

"Well, if you and Drulf can tip that thing over, I can try to push it with the sands. I just need more of its body surface to work with."

Drulf stepped forward. "Let me and the little man see what we can do. Come on."

The blistering sun was already cooking the contents of the scorpion's open cavity. The smell was sickly sweet. Gaeron choked. No telling what this beast would smell like in a day or two. Thankfully, they would be far away by then. Its blood ran in rivulets to form tiny pools in the sand, which were absorbed almost immediately.

Already, a distant vulture cried for its approaching meal.

The two men squatted, using the arachnid's legs for leverage, and heaved. They rocked the scorpion slowly at first, gaining momentum with each iteration. Drulf's pale skin flushed. Gaeron smirked.

"What?" the big Buk Toh said.

Gaeron cocked his chin. "Nice to see you gain some color, that's all."

Drulf grunted. "I'm. Working. This. Thing. Is. Heavy."

"Think I need to get you on the training field again."

"Not. All. Have. Strength. To. Move. Mountains. Ga—Ga"

"Stop talking, and actually start lifting," Gaeron said, already feeling the bloodlust flush from his muscles. Before long, he'd only have the strength of ten men. Best to finish this work now.

Behind them, Chali whispered a chant as she conjured. Just as they exposed the scorpion's back, it was flipped onto its stomach. In a flash, both men fell into the sand, nearly on top of the flattened rider.

Drulf yelped and rolled away, digging at his belt for his sword. Gaeron looked over his shoulder, toward the Chaos Bender. "Really?"

Chali laughed, a brown hand on her flat stomach. "My apologies. But you must admit, that was fun. I guess this is where you thank me."

Pushing himself to his knees, Gaeron gawked. "For what?"

"For helping, of course," Chali said, pointing at the scorpion. "Imagine how much longer you would have struggled with that had I not toppled the stupid creature for you. Now, let's see what he has on him. Maybe he's just robbed a caravan or looted some settlement. For your sake, let's hope your little squashing trick didn't bury anything good in the sands. I'm not digging, if so. That's on you."

Except for a few trinkets, the rider carried little. They took what they thought might have value, which was little more than coin and a dagger with more decorative than practical purposes. They then set out west again, this time with a more wary eye for anyone or anything the countless dunes might hold. Where there was one Scorpion Rider, there were others. The cowards never traveled far without their pack.

Without mounts the village could ill afford to lend them, the going was slower than he liked. They had covered another ten miles, nearly out of the dunes and to the eternal flat of the Olka-Fa desert, when Gaeron pulled up. "What's that?" he said, pointing to the western horizon.

Drulf squinted. "I don't see anything."

"I think I can," Chali said, moving slightly in front him. When she passed, her scent tickled his nose.

By the gods, how did she smell so good? Still?

"On the horizon."

Her head slid forward, as if along an invisible plane. Even with the awkward stance, she was stunning. "Oh, the cloud?"

"Yes."

The Buk Toh threw his hands up, letting them slap his thighs. "I don't see a thing."

"You're blind." Gaeron side-stepped to him, holding his arm level to the horizon. "A black cloud. There. See how far it stretches?"

"That's a cloud? I thought that was a mountain range," the Buk Toh said.

"Another sandstorm, probably." Chali's dark tone hinted she wasn't fooling herself or the two Bound Boys in the party. The most gorgeous woman in Olma-Ka put her water skin to her full lips and drank deeply. A trail of water ran from the corner of her mouth, down her cheek and neck. She pulled the water skin away, cupped her hand and filled it. She ran her wet hand through her hair, pasting a small band of it to her head.

Gaeron cast a sideways glance, and she gave him a coy look. "What?"

He shrugged, his massive shoulders rolling, stretching with relief as the bloodlust continued to dwindle. Unlike anyone in Olma-Ka, his bloodlust was resilient. Whereas most Olmarians felt the surge of power that drove their courage, Gaeron's supplied him with a sense of invincibility. When born, his bloodlust always threatened to override his senses, his mind. The Paramount had told him how he shared that with his mother. They had been friends, and she occasionally told him stories of her personality. Nydera Alethero said his mother often found trouble because of her bloodlust, and that he would too, if he didn't learn how to manage it. The problem was, his bloodlust was too strong to be managed. Too easy to be born to life. Too robust to fade easily.

After so long crossing the Olka-Fa, and the surprise ambush by the Scorpion Rider, a moment of levity felt good.

"I'm surprised to see you be so careless with your water considering we're heading into that," Gaeron said, pointing at the darkened sky. "My instincts tell me that does not bode well for us."

The three—a Chaos Bender, paladin, and warrior—fell quiet as they watched the wall of sky-bound black roll and swirl, never seeming to approach or retreat. No Olmarian had journeyed into the Dark Sands in at least a generation, definitely not during Gaeron's lifetime. In fact, Nydera, the Paramount of Olma-Ka who sent them on this journey, couldn't recall the last time one of their people had attempted the trek. Even Leonaime Nynar, the most knowledgeable Olmarian Gaeron knew, was clueless when the last Olmarian foot had touched the Dark Sands, and she knew everything.

Looking toward the ominous cloud hanging above the desert, Gaeron understood why. They had crossed the Sweet Waters River yesterday. As the desert stretched to the west, they might still have another one or two to go. As the flat land stretched away, and the storm over the horizon blocked out the world, distance was impossible to determine.

Desert life was a harsh life, but Olmarians had carved theirs out and established a vibrant settlement in the village of Olma-Ka. Their people were secure and stable, never wanting much as long as they were responsible with their resources. Theirs was a simpler life that provided freedom to roam and connect with the gods.

Looking at the expanding black hanging over the horizon, Gaeron couldn't think of any people living under that and having those very things he enjoyed. Though ancient peoples had lived here, they no longer did. No one did. The eternal cloud beckoned and repulsed life all at once.

A fat hand slapped him on the back, breaking his reverie. "Don't let it frighten you, little friend. I'm here to protect you.

Plus, we just need to find the Crown of Spikes. Once we've done that, we can get out of here as fast as possible. Which," Drulf said, his chubby cheeks expanding as he loosed a breath toward the black cloud, "I am more than okay with, by the way. The sooner we find the crown, the better. For all the trouble that storm promises, the Paramount better raise us to Three-Marked, let me tell you."

"For one mission where you fought off a single Scorpion Rider and maybe a desert fox?" Chali said with a chuckle. She corked her water skin and slung it around her slender neck.

"We haven't found it yet," Drulf said with a jerk of his chin toward the storm. "Who knows what mysteries await. I, for one, think we will have plenty of chances to earn a Mark. Then we can enjoy becoming Freed." He pulled his own water skin around his neck and drank without bothering to pull the strap over his head.

"And what would you do as a Freed man, Drulf Bural?" Chali said, her lips quirking in a way that hinted she was ready to tease him regardless of his response.

"Careful what you say," Gaeron said.

Drulf's top lip expanded downward, pulling his nose thinner. "I well, uh, well. I—see—"

Chali burst out laughing. The sound of a bird's song to Gaeron's ears.

Chali looked north, toward the mountain range called the Spikes rising above the desert. "The way Nydera tells it, if we're successful, you might not receive your Mark and become Freed, but you won't be simple Bound Boys anymore. The crown will change the fortunes of all Olmarians. Forever."

Gaeron knew she was teasing, but the comment soured his mood. It reminded him how his undeserving brother was already a Two-Marked Freed man, while he was still bound. That made him, made all Bound Boys, a lesser status in the village, no matter what anyone said to the contrary. If he'd done anything over the past few moon cycles, he had proven himself as more than someone who was bound. Heat colored his words. "How can a simple crown do that? A crown is a crown. All queens and blasted kings have them. They're not that unique. If it was special, someone would have found it long ago. Even the Scorpion Riders have had hundreds of years to steal it, since they're the only ones dumb enough to come out here."

"Except us," Drulf said.

"We're blood in the sand," Gaeron said. Even though he knew Drulf was simply trying to pull him out of his darkening mood, no Olmarians should question the Paramount's orders. Even if executing them wouldn't bring a Mark.

"The crown of the Desert King is more than a simple crown," Chali said. "It's said to not only have the rarest of jewels embedded in it, but also magical properties."

"And you believe that?" Gaeron asked. "Magic, held in a crown? That sounds strange. Highly unlikely. Of anyone, I'd figure a Chaos Bender would be more skeptical."

She shrugged. "Possibly. How would I know for sure? At least until I set my eyes on it. But the stories say it is true. The Desert King's crown was the most glorious of its time and has been lost since his people fought the War For the Spikes."

"That war wiped out the first people of the Dark Sands," Drulf said.

Chali nodded. "The Bortellese. Their people, their culture, everything disappeared after the war as the Desert King claimed the Dark Sands as his."

"I remember my father saying something about this part of the desert not actually being dead like it is now," Drulf said, almost too cheerily. "That's why it's black, he said. Hadn't always been. Not until the Desert King. Not only did he kill the people of this region, but their land too."

"That's the way I understand it too," Chali said. "I guess it started during his reign."

"A hundred years, or something like that," Drulf said before turning to Gaeron. "Bet you didn't know that."

"No, because I'm usually too busy working or at weapons training. As a warrior should be. Not sitting around a campfire or the bathing pool, listening to stories. That makes you soft." Gaeron winked and poked Drulf's gut. His finger sank to the first knuckle.

Drulf returned the wink and poked, stabbing Gaeron's temple. "And always playing with blades and not reading makes you soft in the head. But then, I don't suppose a walking pile of muscle has much energy to feed his brain."

Gaeron laughed along with his quick-witted friend. "But, seriously. A hundred-year reign? Impossible."

"Maybe. But if the stories are correct about his magical abilities, then maybe not," Chali replied. "Plus, the day I listen to a warrior about the validity of magical properties of a crown is the day I give up bending Chaos and take up needlework."

"You'd probably be less annoying if you did," Gaeron teased.

Chali gave him a playful shove. But it was she who stumbled, unable to move his mass. Drulf guffawed.

"You just might need this warrior to help you find this crown," Gaeron reminded her.

"Oh, I don't doubt that. It is said the Dark Sands is a dangerous place. So I'm happy to have you along. For now."

"I'll be interested to see what actually lives in the dead desert," Drulf said. "I've read the stories and listened to the elders, but I'm not so sure we'll run into half the things they claim we will."

Chali wagged a finger at him. "Don't be too quick to come to that conclusion, my large friend. You're the only one among us with healing properties. If you are reckless or dismissive of what might be out there, you're screwed."

"He's screwed anyway," Gaeron said.

Though her wide eyebrows pinched, Chali continued, ignoring him. "The way I understand it, once the Bortellese were slaughtered by the Desert King, he died not too soon after. It's said his ghost never left the Black Palace."

"Ghost? No such thing," Gaeron said.

"I can't believe my fate rests in the hands of someone who believes in nothing," Chali sighed, only half–serious.

"I believe in things, though" Drulf said, drawing out the last word as if he was stumbling over a foreign tongue.

"Oh, I know. But, then again, you always were smarter than Gaeron"

"Sure, things like ammits, babites. Scorpion riders." Gaeron rocked his head. "Those are things to believe in."

"As opposed to?"

"Ghosts of dead kings."

Drulf nodded, the loose skin under his chin jiggling. "If I've seen them, then they're real. If I've read multiple accounts of something I've never seen, I'll at least entertain thoughts it could be real. But if I only hear stories? Well... I'll be much more careful. I mean, have you ever heard Bound Boys talk about what the first thing they'll do to a Freed woman once their bands are cut?"

Gaeron smirked, dropping and shaking his head.

"Exactly," Drulf said with a beaming smile. "Stories are just harder to believe. That's all. But I won't discount them."

"I might," Gaeron admitted.

"So, you're telling me that if you've never seen something, your default is that it cannot be real?" Chali asked.

Gaeron remained quiet. The Chaos Bender was leading him into a dangerous question, and he wanted no part of it. If Drulf decided to play along, that was on him. Gaeron would leave him on his own. Chali was more than a match for both of them, and Gaeron wasn't about to let her pin him down. She'd remind him of that every single new sun, if he did.

He only remained quiet for another half mile. "Come on,

Chali. You can't honestly believe in fairytales and children's stories. You're a..."

Chali raised an eyebrow. "A what?"

Drulf gave Gaeron a shake of his head, pinching his mouth like he'd just been forced to eat a bitterberry tart.

Gaeron shrugged. "I just meant to say that, as a Chaos Bender, you should be careful what you choose to believe in. Have some proof or something."

"Like?"

He tapped the sword at his hip. "Blades. They're sharp and strong. They break, slice, and cut. Some are more durable than others. Some are blunt, while others could cut the air. Understanding the nature of the variety of blades could take a lifetime of study. As a Chaos Bender, wouldn't it be better to spend your time studying what you know is real instead of entertaining so many what-ifs and maybes? That's all."

"If I only believed in things I could touch, smell, taste, or see, I wouldn't be prepared for battle half the time. I definitely wouldn't possess a number of Chaos spells I enjoy, not any of those I've created myself," Chali said. She fell silent, her eyes on the growing dark cloud gripping the approaching horizon. Even though they'd set a demanding pace, that storm still appeared locked over the land where they'd first spotted it. "There are things we don't understand which hide in the corners of the world. The Paramount included you two in this mission because she knows you possess the skills all Olmarians should have. Should, not do. There's a difference. You set the example for others to follow. You are leaders, whether you want to think of yourselves as such or not."

"We're not leaders," Gaeron said. "We're Bound Boys. Nothing more."

Chali pulled up, grabbing Gaeron's forearm. Her touch was almost a caress instead of a grip. Her chasmal eyes were hard as they searched his, as if she were trying to read his deepest thoughts. The ends of her hair, pulled up in the

Warrior's Embrace, wagged in the slight breeze that did nothing to cool the day. "Do you really see yourself as nothing more than a Bound Boy, Gaeron Andel?"

"That is all I am," he said.

She held his wrist for a moment before drawing a long breath and releasing her hold. When she spoke, her gaze went back to the dark cloud as if she were speaking to it. "Well then, I hope before we return to Olma-Ka, you have changed your mind. I have a feeling whatever waits for us at the end of this journey will change it for you if you don't. Not only you, but you as well, Drulf. All of us. I see it."

Drulf's face scrunched. "See what?"

She popped one shoulder up. "When they tell the stories of our lives around the Circle of Fire many sun cycles from now, I think the people they'll speak of will sound like strangers to us. Whatever the gods have planned to challenge us with, here, in the Black Palace, beyond the days when we returned to Olma-Ka, we'll need to change who we are to be ready to deal with it."

2

GAERON

THE DARK CLOUD swallowed the sun.

Gaeron wrapped his arms around himself as a chill settled on his skin. Beside him, Chali's teeth clattered as she shivered. She'd even pulled her dark hair out of the Warrior's Embrace and let it drape over her shoulders. Gaeron left his long braids in the topknot, though the back of his neck prickled. Even Drulf, who had more than a fair share of body fat to insulate him, walked with his arms wrapping his cloak tightly around his torso.

"I don't think even Hastelle was this cold," the large Buk Toh said.

"It wasn't." Gaeron squinted toward where the sun should have hung, bright and blazing. Instead, he could only make out a faint outline of the glowing orb behind the dark cloud. "I've never seen anything like this."

"Nor I," Chali said, her voice as chilled as the air.

Only the day before, they had been sweating under that desert sun. Once they passed underneath the dark cloud that grew as they neared and never seemed to move, the air chilled and the desert sounds died. The cold was awful; as people of the Olka-Fa desert, a day without sun was rare.

Gaeron remembered only a handful of gray days in his entire life except for the times he'd traveled south.

Stretching to the west, north, and south as far as he could see, it seemed as if all life was repulsed by this region.

"I don't like it," Drulf said, looking skyward.

"The way it moves, but…" Chali started.

Gaeron understood. "But there is no wind."

From the ground up, the storm choked out the rest of the world.

Not an agave or buckhorn sprout. No hedgehog or brittle-bush. Not even a single cactus. What the storm kissed, it had killed.

The silence after entering the Dark Sands was nearly as troubling as the swirling storm. Gaeron had yet to hear a single snake hiss or rattle. It was as if the hovering, rolling mass of black above them had chased even the hardiest of life out of the Dark Sands. In fact, the only sound he'd heard was the cracking of the black sand under his feet, as if he walked on brittle wood.

"Well, look at it this way," Drulf said, breaking the silence. "There is nothing here, so it shouldn't be hard to find the crown. First, we just have to find something that might have been used for secure storage. Or, I guess, palatial, kingly ruins. Which reminds me, are we sure we're headed in the right direction?"

Gaeron defaulted to Chali, who spent the moon cycle before they left Olma-Ka preparing spells and herself. She'd thoroughly analyzed maps and read up on the entire history of the region while recovering from a severe injury. Of anyone in the party who might have a confident answer to the question, it was her.

"I hope we'll find buildings soon enough," she finally answered Drulf. "The Borttel ruins are supposed to be just north of the Black Palace. We will have to search both, in most likelihood. If you really want to search inside buildings, you'll get the chance." Her eyes danced skyward, analyzing. "In all honesty, I'm looking forward to it. I don't wish to be out in this any longer than I have to be. I want something with cover, preferably made from stone so we can build a fire."

"Ha, with what?" Gaeron flicked his hand at a nondescript point in the distance, because here, everything was nondescript. "There's little to burn. It'll take us a full day to scrape enough to get through a single sleeping sun. Plus, with places like ruins and something called the Black Palace? Are you sure you wouldn't rather be out in the open desert?" Gaeron's mind flashed back to the Hastelle mission. That city, with looming stone walls, tall homes, and an immense palace, had suffocated him. During that mission to abduct a merchant who owed a debt to Olmarians, they'd remained in the streets and the crowded marketplace. They'd only entered one home, which served as a headquarters of sorts, and that'd been enough for him. Nothing about being closed in was enticing. Tents were fine. They bent with the desert winds. Stone piled around and above? Maybe he'd propose protecting their rear from the outside if they ever found one of these places? Being inside a palace sounded like absolute torture, no matter how grand.

Chali waved at the black storm. "Better than being stuck out in this at night. We can guess this is permanent. The stories say so. It hasn't moved since you spotted it, so I doubt it's going anywhere. So we need to. I don't want to be out in the elements if this is as good as it gets."

Now Drulf seemed locked on that swirling mass above. "This, at night? No thanks. I agree that it's not a storm. Not a natural one. I think this is as much a part of the Dark Sands as the ground we walk on."

"I can't believe there was ever a Desert King who slaughtered an entire people for the right to rule this," Gaeron said, a bitter taste on his lips.

Chali said, "The stories say it wasn't always like this,

though. This," she said, gesturing around them, "is what became of the Dark Sands as a result of the magic he used to destroy the Borttelese and build the Black Palace. Before then, this part of the desert looked very much like what we know. This is what great magic does if those who cast the spells can't or won't contain them."

A silence fell on the party, joining that of the dead desert. If magic did this to such a vast region, how powerful had the Desert King been? If he was capable of such significant works, could Chali also be one day? Could she undo this? The Dark Sands was said to stretch to the western ends of the desert, but Gaeron knew that was a lie. People from a village called Ol-ta had traded with his people before. Years had passed since he'd seen one in the village, but he remembered them because of the way their dark skin matched Olmarians, slightly lighter than the Sun Skinned Scorpion Riders. So the Dark Sands wasn't endless, just immense. If Chali could one day end the spell that kept this region captive to this death storm, the Olmarians could regenerate the land and expand westward, opening routes to new people. Maybe she had entertained that thought as well. If so, that explained her fascination with the Desert King and this region of Oltari he had sucked the life from.

After they broke for their meal, they restarted their journey, refreshed. His restored senses helped him pick up a large shape in the distance some time later. "Is that..."

Chali squinted at the gigantic rectangular shape. "The Black Palace."

"That's where we search first?" Drulf asked, his Adam's apple bobbing as he swallowed.

Chali nodded. "It's the best chance we have of finding this crown. I think—" Chali pulled up short. "Listen. Do you hear that?"

Gaeron stopped to listen. Without wind, bird chirps and songs, or even the scurrying of desert animals underneath the sand, the dead air made it easy to pick up the strange clacking and clattering.

"Something is rattling, but that's no snake," Drulf said in a hush.

Gaeron said, "I don't see anything."

"But you hear it, right?" Chali asked. "It's not just Drulf and me who are going crazy?"

He nodded. "Any ideas what it is?"

The Chaos Bender bit her lip but said nothing. Gaeron noted that she had freed her hands of her water skin and pulled the robe sleeves back.

He focused on the rattling, picking out its general direction. Without life, without buildings to bounce sound off, he didn't have difficulty pinpointing what he heard. "I don't like this." He slid the two-headed ax from his back and held it diagonally.

Drulf eyed his battleax before searching Gaeron's face. "What's going on?"

"I don't know," Gaeron said, giving Drulf a quick shake of his head. "But whatever it is, I'm going to be ready for it."

The big paladin didn't need further evidence. He glanced at the Chaos Bender's rolled sleeves and freed hands, back at Gaeron's ax, and then unsheathed his own weapon, a shortsword.

As Gaeron stepped between Chali and the sound, she shot him a look. Concern? Determination? Was she pissed he was doing what the Paramount had sent him to accomplish? She could get over that. As a Chaos Bender, Chali performed poorly in physical confrontations. The danger in crossing her came from her ability to use the environment to weave spells. Doing so required her full focus. To do that, he and Drulf needed to serve as buffers to any threats.

"Let's move closer," Gaeron suggested.

Drulf cleared his throat. "I only hear it from that direction."

He pointed due west. "We could circumnavigate the area, go to the south or north, and avoid trouble altogether."

"If we avoid trouble now, it might find us at a worse time. Like when we're sleeping," Chali said.

Gaeron shook his head and spoke up before his friend could answer. "It's already getting late. We have no shelter except for that." He cocked his head toward the Black Palace. "At this pace, we wouldn't make it before nightfall. It's too far. We can't go back. There's no shelter behind us, and this crown is before us... somewhere. I say we press on, see what this noise is, and deal with anything we need to deal with. Then we can find a place to rest for the night. If we're hearing something, then the desert holds life. Life requires some sort of shelter." He looked up at the black cloud of dust that scoured the sky, hoping his friend saw the sense in his position.

Chali considered a moment longer. "I'm in favor. Drulf?"

He cocked his head to look down at the party leader without taking his gaze away from the source of the rattling. "You're the leader, Chali. You tell us what your decision is."

"I want your input," she said.

"You sure about this?" Drulf asked Gaeron, who nodded.

With a sigh that expanded his round chest, Drulf huffed. "Okay. Let's go."

The party started forward. The rattling turned from dull to a clear clacking and clattering, accompanied by deeper thuds. A cacophony. Too many noises to be created by a single, industrious creature. To Gaeron, this almost sounded like... a settlement.

"What is that?" Drulf said, shifting his shortsword in his meaty hands.

"Let's find out." Gaeron didn't wait for an answer from Drulf or approval from Chali.

With his battleax gripped, he cocked it to a striking pose with a quarter-turn and crept forward. The terrain sloped just enough to obscure the source. Gaeron counted the strides as they approached. He wanted to be sure he knew how far sound carried in the dead desert. Surprised, he only reached fifty before the desert fell away into a pit. He took an involuntary step backward, jerking the battleax higher.

Drulf gasped, and Chali let out a low moan. They had stepped back as well.

"This is trouble," the Chaos Bender whispered.

Drulf mumbled something inaudible.

Gaeron growled as his body heated with the first blossom of bloodlust, sparked not by a fight or threat, but merely from the presence of the creatures below.

"Nobody said anything about... well, anything like... like this," Drulf said.

"I don't think anyone knows," Chali said, staring down at the horror.

The flat desert had obstructed this immense pit until they stumbled upon it. Had they been a mile to the north or south, they would have passed by without a clue.

The pit had been trenched from the desert floor. This dig must have taken a lifetime. With walls so sheer that he still feared falling even though he stood fifteen feet away, the pit descended eighty feet. The oval was larger than the city of Hastelle. Had the gods plunked the city in the middle of this pit, the only thing visible would have been the tops of its walls and the keep. How many villages like Olma-Ka could be contained here?

"How can no one know about this?" Gaeron asked no one in particular.

"Maybe it's newly constructed?" Drulf offered.

"By who? The Desert King was the last to live in the Dark Sands, I thought?" Gaeron said.

"He was." Chali's voice was haunted.

Gaeron understood. The pit that swallowed this section of

desert was unsettling. What moved along the flat floor was worse.

"Looks like the children's stories are true," Drulf intoned.

Skinless. Hundreds of moving skeletons. The pit was so populated by them, they constantly bumped into one another as they ambled aimlessly. The bare bones clanked as they moved. Even those who rocked in place seemed to contribute to the rattling buzz. No skin. No muscle or ligaments. Just naked bone, darkened only by the Dark Sands storm and time.

"By the gods, this is grotesque," Drulf said as he took in the scene.

"Do you think they're what's left of the people the Desert King destroyed?" Gaeron asked the Chaos Bender.

Chali blinked. Her eyes focused on something more than the city of animated skeletons.

A city of skeletons, held at bay, maybe even as prisoners, only by deep walls. Every size, from the height of a child to some who, even from this vantage point, were taller than Drulf. They moved in jerky motions. Constant motion. None of them bore the rags or riches of their former mortal lives. Stripped clean of clothes, skin, ligaments and muscle, shed of all remnants of what they once were.

These poor people, victims of ancient wars, couldn't find rest even after death. Gaeron's lips drew apart in a snarl. The dead ruler deserved whatever fate befell him for sealing his subjects in this eternity.

"Ghastly," Chali said. She pulled her eyes away from the pit, surveying their surroundings. "Looks like we're taking the long way around."

Drulf snorted.

Gaeron tipped his head toward the Black Palace to the south. "This way?"

"The only option. Unless you're planning to tour every grain of the Olka-Fa?" the Chaos Bender said.

South-bound, they made their way around the pit. Gaeron watched the Skinless below. None seemed cognizant of the living beings above them. His bloodlust began to abate as he contemplated the eternal misery the creatures suffered. Alive, but not. Dead, but not. Oglatuu, the god of life essence, was cruel to allow this in the first place; to force these creatures to suffer for generations was unconscionable. Best to put this pit and the decayed creatures where they belonged; in the past.

Drulf broke the silence. "That has to be an entire city of people."

"Borttel was said to be the largest city in the desert. Well, before the Desert King invaded," Chali said. "You both were in Hastelle and saw what that was like. Borttel was equal, supposedly."

"A prison," Gaeron interjected.

"It's what they know," Chali said with the wisdom of her extra half decade of living. "I imagine that was what it was like for these people. It would be interesting to see how they lived, wouldn't it?"

Gaeron wasn't sure he agreed.

"I, for one, think—" Drulf yelped.

Gaeron spun in time to see his friend slip.

They had been walking along the edge of the pit because, Gaeron figured, they felt better monitoring the horde of Skinless. Maybe Drulf hadn't been paying attention. Maybe the sand underneath him gave way. Whatever the reason, the big man's foot shot downward.

Gaeron dove, snagging the large man by the arm.

The Buk Toh's eyes were wide. "Don't let go of me, you little bastard."

"I won't," Gaeron grunted, trying to edge away from the pit. His booted feet dug into the sand. Had the Buk Toh worn gauntlets, Gaeron could have used those for a better grip. The man's clammy forearms provided little more than another problem to overcome.

"The desert never yields," Olmarians were found of saying. Yet now that wasn't true. As Gaeron dug his feet in to pull his friend to safety, the sands gave way underneath him. Without firm ground to brace against, Drulf pulled him closer to the pit instead of Gaeron pulling them both away.

Gaeron was remotely aware of Chali, close and conjuring. Below Drulf, a cloud of sand formed in the air. As Chali chanted, Gaeron pulled futilely. Drulf did his part, trying to find purchase on the cliff side. So far, their efforts were in vain.

Below, the clattering intensified. Gaeron tried to ignore the Skinless. He pulled, heaved. Drulf was the larger man by half a foot and fifty pounds, but he didn't bear Gaeron's strength. No one in Olma-Ka did. He couldn't help himself as much as Gaeron could.

Digging his heels into the sand, pushing more and more away, Gaeron found firmer purchase. He adjusted his grip on Drulf's arm, alternating hands to claim more and more of it as he lifted the bigger man. Finally, he clasped his friend's armpit. One foot slipped, and he nearly lost his grasp, but regained it before everything was lost.

"Chali, do something!" Drulf cried.

Gaeron wrapped his hand as far under Drulf as he could and yanked, pulling in small increments at a time.

"I am!" Chali shouted. Her hands moved more hastily.

Around Drulf, sand swirled as if being pushed by different air streams. Swirling tighter and constricting into circles. The vortexes coalesced, solidifying and blocking out anything that lay beyond or below.

The Skinless rattled and knocked. The clatter of their unnatural irritation worried Gaeron as he pulled. Chali's sand wall slid lower into the pit. Gaeron feared her spell had broken. Right now, he couldn't worry about that. Saving Drulf required every ounce of his focus.

"I feel it on my feet!" Drulf exclaimed. "I can feel it! It's solid, Chali. Solid as rock."

"Then come out of there."

Gaeron watched a stupid smile spread on his friend's face, and then Drulf was standing, pulling his arm free of Gaeron's grasp. The pit edge reached nearly to his biceps, but Drulf looked nothing but tickled by the experience.

"What... how?" Gaeron stumbled to form the question.

Drulf raised his arms skyward, standing as if on the air itself.

Behind him, Chali snickered. "Well, that worked as well as I had hoped it would. That's the first time I've built a platform from sand. Glad to see I didn't screw it up."

"Me too," Drulf said, as he pulled himself out of the pit and back to the desert floor. "Even though I never expected you to screw up anything. Just so you know."

Gaeron took a second to peek over the edge of the pit at Chali's sand platform. Impressive, he had to admit. It looked solid and had to have been to support Drulf's weight. Still, he reached to feel it for himself when Chali's spell broke.

Behind him, Drulf said, "That was amazing."

Gaeron didn't care about his friend's thoughts. He rocketed to his feet, shoving the pair forward, away from the pit. "Be ready!"

Drulf's lips quivered. He shook his head, as if trying to clear it. "Wha—what?"

Gaeron snatched his battleax. "They're climbing! Out! The Skinless are coming."

"Shit!" Drulf scrambled to draw his shortsword while Chali stepped back, her hands raising as she weaved a new spell.

"They must have seen us!" Gaeron spread his feet to form a solid base. He stood within a body's length of the pit's edge. Running into the desert would be futile unless the Skinless could not navigate the sand. Nothing about their movements in the pit told him they couldn't handle this terrain. Plus, if they were the animated skeletons of the Bortellese, then this was their land. They would know it better than the trio ever could.

"How close," Chali asked.

"Very."

When Chali's platform spell had ended, removing the obstruction, the first sight of the pit Gaeron had was a tower of skeletons building to the pit's edge. Sometime while saving Drulf, the Skinless noticed and were coming for them. One stood on another's shoulders. Then another. Then another. And another. The skeletons climbed on and supported each other until they reached the ledge.

The small party slunk back as the first hand clawed at the edge.

As the skeleton pulled itself up, Gaeron sprinted forward and swung the battleax, separating its head from its body. The skeleton flew backwards, over the empty air.

But he didn't have time to revel. Another skeleton was climbing out. Drulf took that one's head off. Then another. Then another. Then another.

The two men took turns swinging and decapitating skeletons as they attempted to breach the pit. Chali conjured from the rear. The skeletons were coming so fast now that he and Drulf were a constant blur. Swinging, killing, and swinging again.

Horrified, Gaeron noticed another tower of skeletons twenty feet away.

A third was reaching the ledge far beyond Drulf's right. A fourth was sprouting from the pit floor, just beyond the third. Those breaching the pit now ran at the trio.

"Drop back! Protect Chali," he ordered his friend.

Drulf raced to stand in front of the Chaos Bender. He took out skeletons as fast as he could while Gaeron held the first tower at bay. He had to help Drulf before he was swarmed. But how? This one tower kept his full attention.

Around the pit, the dark sands swirled in chaotic tangles. Completely encircling the pit, it was as if the black cloud hovering over this region had fallen.

"Gaeron! Back up. To me," Chali ordered.

"I've got to stop them coming out," Gaeron shouted over the growing tumult of wind and whipping sand.

"Now, you bonehead!" Chali shouted. "I'm trying to blind them. I can't do that with you in the way."

Gaeron took the head off the next skeleton and reluctantly sprinted at Chali. Drulf was taking slow, deliberated steps backward, one step at a time as he swung his shortsword to take off arms, legs, and heads. Chali was trying to move back while casting.

Together again, the trio slowly backed away, fighting off skeletons as they closed in.

Chali shot Gaeron a sideways glance as she pulled her truncheon free. Chaos Benders couldn't use edged weapons, the elders said. Something about the nature of their gifts couldn't be combined with edged blades. Gaeron never paid much attention to the stories. Faced with so many skeletons, he was almost willing to have Chali test the stories. "That storm will continue to grow for a while. It'll keep the rest of them in the pit, but not forever. We need to go."

But they couldn't go. Thirty. Forty. Fifty skeletons charged them at wild speeds. They flung themselves at the mortals. Drulf caught two and smashed them together, breaking them as if they were porcelain. Gaeron lifted his battleax, swinging it in a high, constant circle to keep the skeletons at bay. Chali danced with the few who broke through. By the sounds of the thunks behind him, her truncheon worked as he hoped it would against the skeletons.

Just when it felt like the sea of skeletons would never end, Gaeron slashed and dashed another three. Finishing the breaking of the piles of bones, his bloodlust, muted. Huffing, he waited for more, but nothing came from underneath the swirling cloud of black sand.

"Let's go," Chali said. "I don't know how much longer my storm will hold. Once we're far enough away, it will fall. Best to put as much distance between us and the pit as we can while there's still light and I still have the energy. Let's head north. That's the shortest route around the pit now. I don't care if we have to take the long way to the palace, as long as it's away from here."

Gaeron used the head of the battleax to point at the piles of bones around his feet. "But we've defeated them. We can head south, toward the Black Palace and have cover."

Chali shook her head. "No. The stories are very clear about the Skinless. At nightfall, they will regenerate."

"Regenerate?"

She bit her lip before answering. "Yes. Reform. I don't know if it's true or not. But are you two willing to take that chance? After such a long day, I can't guarantee you I could cast another spell that large. I might not be able to save us if they come back. We would have to fight the entire pit without my strongest spells. Is that what you want?"

Neither man checked for the other's perspective.

"No," they said in unison.

Their synchronicity solidified the decision, and the party ran a sweeping path around the pit. Gaeron placed himself between Drulf and the hidden edge.

"I'm so glad your clumsy ass came along," he joked after the pit had fallen behind them. Joking helped him feel better about what he saw now in the distance. The magical seal Chali conjured still encased it, but it was thinning. "Would have been boring without you."

"Without me you wouldn't have had that practice with your ax," Drulf laughed. "And, trust me, the way you fought back there, you need all the practice you can get."

3

NEVILAN

"Do you think they can be trusted?" Rercan asked from Nevilan's side.

Without taking his eyes off the work crew, Nevilan allowed himself a calculated smile. Things were falling into place. The pace was frustratingly slow, but he had to admit, it worked in his favor. "If they're smart, they won't say a word."

"And if they're not? What then?" came the pointed response from his pointy-chinned friend.

West, across the planting fields, Nevilan watched the farmers toil in the best soil Olma-Ka had in this otherwise hard landscape. Bent over, except for the occasional break to stretch backs and wipe sweat from foreheads, they worked strenuously. In the foreground, men worked at the bottom of the ditch, expanding it northward, around the west side of the village. They'd made steady progress over the past few days, but another five moon cycles would pass before they finished.

That was fine with Nevilan. As long as they worked on the project, he had time to influence others. That's what this was about. Time with them, away from the ears of Freed women. As a Two-Marked Freed man, Nevilan used his social rank to separate men he trusted into a smaller crew. He needed them alone. Now they were. The watchful eyes of the Freed woman in the northwest watchtower scanned the ditch diggers when she bored of watching the horizon for threats. Whenever her analysis drifted his way, he was careful to appear engaged. When her attention returned to her primary duty, he influenced.

This was backbreaking work. The men needed breaks, and it was during those breaks that he planted seeds that would sprout questions.

Nevilan pinched his lips, answering Rercan, if for no other reason than to fool his friend into thinking his opinions mattered. "We'll root them out then."

"How?" Rercan said, his forearm resting on his shovel. His short, black bangs, parted on one side, lay flattened by sweat against his forehead. He flinched when Nevilan looked at him and cleared his throat. "I mean, how can we do that without drawing attention?"

Nevilan found the question humorous. "We?"

Rercan lips fluttered as he shrugged. "Yes... we—I mean, I thought—"

"You make yourself look more foolish with each word," Tocan Danold said. He was six-feet tall and as thin as a cottonwood reed. His face looked like an eagle's, framed by long, slick curls. The shadow of facial hair made him look ten years older than his true age.

"No one asked you, Tocan," Rercan said, moving his arm from the shovel and extending it as if he were trying to broaden himself.

Tocan stepped forward. "This may come as a surprise to you, Rercan, but you're not the only one who can provide perspective and guidance to Nevilan. I can as well. In fact, I'm more qualified than you."

"How so?" Rercan asked, but Nevilan interrupted any coming response.

"What makes you think I requested or even need your

guidance, Tocan?" He enjoyed knocking the taller man down. Tocan had a look about him that gave the impression he knew things no one else did. He was now, and would continue to be, a good servant to Nevilan's plans. Yet, he needed his wings clipped from time to time, lest he think he could fly above superior men. "The way I see it, I benefit from listening to voices I trust. Those of wisdom. The pair of you can spend your time squabbling, or you can spend your time observing and learning."

Chastised, Tocan dipped his head, wisely remaining silent. Rercan had eyes only for his rival, slowly lifting his pointed chin in unearned victory.

"For example," Nevilan said, waving an open palm at the Bound Boys digging into the desert, "which of them would you trust to help us?"

Rercan and Tocan looked along the line of silent, sweaty Olmarian men.

"Those two. Janes, as well, of course," Tocan answered first, picking out the broad Bound Boy Nevilan was very familiar and comfortable with, and two larger Bound Boys. A hardworking threesome, to be sure.

Janes Firon had just passed his twenty-second sun cycle but was the size of a man ten years his senior. The downward slope of his shoulders swelled as he rocked, moving soil from the ditch and tossing it five feet above to the rim instead of using the wheelbarrows like everyone else. Nevilan nodded. Youth and energy were a dangerous combination. As the day dragged on, everyone slowed, but not Janes. Nevilan couldn't remember the broad man taking a break.

One of the other pair, was an even bigger, broader man. But young. Maybe too young. Plus, the way he lumbered as he worked outlined immediate concerns. Someone like him would have a limited skill set. The last looked too stupid to understand which direction the sun woke.

"And you, Rercan?" Nevilan asked.

Rercan took longer to answer. He glanced up and down the line numerous times. "I agree with Janes. He is trustworthy and committed to you. He knows the disrespect you've suffered at the hands of your brother and also understands the threat Gaeron poses, I feel. I would include Welton Ramsik in that equation as well. But those two," Rercan paused to take in two Bound Boys pushing a wheelbarrow up a plank ramp, "I'm not so sure about."

"Why not?" Nevilan asked before Tocan piped in.

Rercan didn't answer immediately. Instead, he watched the two, his expression thoughtful. "We don't know them on that level. I would never think to testify for someone I didn't know well enough to hand a dagger and turn my back on."

A satisfactory answer which Nevilan wouldn't validate. Not now. Not in front of Tocan.

The tall man sneered. "That's why you're an imbecile. Look at the size of those two. The pair alone could handle anyone who causes trouble. Honestly, Nevilan," Tocan said, turning to face him, "I don't know why you take the Council of this twat. He won't advise you appropriately. I'm half convinced he's inclined to put you in danger. Take any words he says with caution."

Rercan opened his mouth, but Nevilan cut them both off. He was finished with their pitiful competition. "You say those two could help our cause, yet they have not shown me anything at this point. Definitely no deference to my word. How do I know they're not complete imbeciles, as you accuse Rercan of being?"

Tocan's face flickered. Doubt, there and gone in a flash.

This one is dangerous. Useful, but dangerous.

Tocan covered his reaction with a hearty laugh. "Simple. We wouldn't be using them for their brains. We need their brawn, that's all."

Nevilan preferred letting the silence keep these two men thinking about his position while he watched the work crew.

Before he asked, he had already determined who he was going to include. Rercan had named two. Tocan, only the obvious choice in Janes. Hardly surprising. Tocan's strength was his devious mind, but he thought like a needle, always progressing in a narrow path. This was yet the latest example.

After another thirty feet of ditch was dug, Nevilan called for a break. Most of the men moved underneath the only shade they had, the shadow of the watchtower. While they did, Nevilan called his council. Rercan, Tocan, Janes, Welton, Yastel Holton, and Hok. The last of them didn't even have a last name, his ancestry originating from somewhere in the western desert. He was nearly as large as the two brutes Tocan had named, but far more intelligent and with a mean streak that would make a Ten-Marked woman quiver. Enough to be useful without being a threat.

They moved from the work site, but not so far as to draw the attention of the scout standing watch in the tower. Too early, far too early to solicit inquiries into his actions, especially by a Freed woman.

He pulled three water skins from the bag he had Tocan carry to the site and disbursed them. The crew took them hesitantly.

"I use my own water skin," Welton said, his hand slipping to his belt where his water skin hung.

Ignoring the Bound Boy's big eyes, like that of a frightened jack rabbit, Nevilan pointed at the new skin. "That's not water. That's wine."

Welton's head shot up. Janes and Yastel shared a look. Hok remained steadfast, watching the conversation with crossed arms as thick as beams. "Wine? Surely you mean mead?"

"No. What I said is what I meant. You'd do well to remember that, Welton. That's wine. A red. From Evelence," Nevilan said, keeping his voice even. He was excited for this power-play, something he'd waited so long to execute. These Bound Boys could not see that excitement. Not yet. Poise and composure now, or he'd wear them down before he called on their passion. Plus, they needed to know from the outset they were not the same as him. He raised his arm, palm facing skyward, in encouraging pulses. "Go ahead. Drink and enjoy. You have earned it. Each of you have. I've been watching, and it is clear you're doing the work of ten men. Why not be rewarded for your efforts?"

"I don't know about that," Janes said. "Rit and Undul are putting in more than their fair share."

"Who are they?" Tocan asked.

Janes tipped his head toward the watchtower, where the rest of the crew sprawled out in the cooler sand. "The two large ones sitting off to the side there. The mountains with feet."

Interesting. Those were the two Tocan had recommended. "They're slow and cumbersome. Men like them eat too much, take too much time, and usually are as intelligent as a mountain, with or without feet." The Bound Boys nervously chuckled. Nevilan found encouragement in that, so he continued. "Not like the lot of you. I've been watching you and I have to say I am impressed. Good men are what Olma-Ka needs, now more than ever."

"Thank you, sir," Yastel Holton said. Exerting as he had, the man's spongy spring of hair stood like tall flames shooting from campfire logs. "My Pa always taught me that a Bound Boy only became a valued man through hard work."

It was a simple sentiment, one that resonated with the type of people he needed to convince. So instead of criticizing the message or messenger, Nevilan pursed his lips and nodded. "A very smart man, it must be said. Good advice. Wise advice that is as true in words as it is in actions. That is why I wanted to gather the six of you. By catching my eye, you have set yourselves apart from the rest of this lot."

Hok's eyes went to Rercan and Tocan, but Nevilan refused to play to the gesture. It wasn't something to address because it would only draw attention from the other three, who had not noticed how much less Rercan and Tocan worked. No, Hok's observation would just have to be noted for now. Maybe the lumbering giant was smarter than Nevilan had given him credit for. Time and opportunity would tell.

"It's just a shame others aren't pulling their weight," Rercan said. "Were the village's work distributed equitably, we could complete it expediently, and it would be less taxing on those who now carry the burden."

Nevilan gave him a nod so deep his chin touched his chest. "Absolutely correct. It's a shame that good men—I refuse to use a derogatory term like Bound Boys for you— must bear the weight of responsibility for all Olmarians."

Interest sparked in Janes's eyes. "What do you mean?"

Nevilan cocked his head. "Do any of you know what this project is? Do you know its full scope?" When the small group cast glances at each other, each unsure, Nevilan continued as Rercan and Tocan played their parts. "We are responsible for digging this ditch around the entire village."

"Completely around Olma-Ka?" Yastel asked.

Nevilan held his eyes. "Completely." He let the response linger.

"Even out by the stables?" Welton asked.

"Even the stables. Around the grove. Running from watch-tower to watchtower." Nevilan swept a hand at the one occupied by the nosy Freed woman just a few hundred feet away.

Janes whistled. "That's going to take moon cycles, maybe longer, if the sun burns too brightly. Look at how it slowed us today."

Rercan agreed. "Imagine how miserable it will be in the middle of the hot season."

"We'll lose good men," Nevilan said in a haunting tone. "Maybe a lot of good men." He looked at all six in turn, stop-ping long enough to ensure they knew he was speaking to them through the shared silence. "Maybe even some of you."

Their reactions were mixed. Fear, trepidation, frustration on Hok's part, and even anger. Each would be tapped into in time.

"Imagine if all Olmarians shared in this responsibility. Not just in this shameful project, but in all work," Nevilan said. "Imagine how a few of the Freed helping would ease this workload. Why shouldn't we? Ever since I earned my first Mark and became Freed, I've been thinking about why we don't contribute as much as the Bound—excuse me—as those not yet deemed Free, I mean. What is it about our station in life that determines we shouldn't have to share in your labor? This project," he said, extending his arms in a grand gesture to both sides, "is not just a ditch. The Paramount plans to build a stockade. She's planning physical defenses for the village, scarring the desert and spitting in the face of Shittara. We have become a people who now fear that which comes from the outside. When has that ever happened in the entire history of Olma-Ka?"

Janes chewed his lip. Hok made a fist. Welton's chest swelled.

"Some things are changing. But too many are not," he continued. "When Nydera Alethero became Paramount, she told us that the old ways would not become the new. But where are these new ways she spoke of? Look around. Who is lifting the shovels? Who is moving the desert? Which Olmarians are sweating under the sun while the Freed women sit in their tents, away from its piercing rays? Who is eating and sleeping and fucking at this very moment while you exhaust yourselves for their comfort?"

Hok growled.

"Are these truly new ways, or are they the old ways mutated to satiate Olmarians? To keep them happy with 'just enough' of this 'new'?" Nevilan asked, allowing his tone to bite. He hung his head, shaking it sadly. "My heart truly breaks at this, sword brothers."

The silence told him the comment hit his target. Someone shuffled their feet. A water skin gurgled.

He reached deep inside, in the dark shadows of his life, where he doubted. The places where he hated himself for not being what his parents wanted, or the twisted shadow of knowledge no one regarded him as highly as his younger brother. His bound brother. He tapped into that raw hatred. Lifting his tear-stained face, he showed the gathered Bound Boys the shame of a Freed man.

"I cry for what you are going through and will continue to experience," he said between sniffles. "I cry for the men we have not lost, but surely will. I cry for your pain, your struggle. I cry because Nydera promised the old ways would not become the new, yet every single one of you still suffers. That includes those men trying to cool their overheated bodies in the shade of a watchtower manned by a Freed woman who sits in the shade all day. The men who have their cocks banded until they prove themselves worthy of an archaic gesture by a barbaric act."

The Bound Boys waited. Chests rose and fell in breaths driven rapid by adrenaline. Enraptured. Even Rercan and Tocan looked stunned by the direction of the conversation. He hadn't prepared them for this because he wanted their reactions to be as raw as the other four. The influence of numbers. That's how people were moved to action.

Hiding his glee was difficult but necessary. None of the men looked away. He had them where he wanted them. "I cry *because* the old ways have become the new." He swallowed, making sure they noticed, before composing himself. This time, his words came out with proud conviction. "And time has come for that to change."

4

NYDERA

KARADEHTI GROANED, wiping her head with the sleeve of her red robe. The silk pushed away more sweat than it absorbed. "It's miserable today."

Nydera Alethero, Paramount of Olma-Ka, didn't disagree with her sword sister. Every Freed woman claimed another who was not only her dearest friend, but also a trusted confidant who could wield a blade, share child-rearing duties, and wipe each other's asses in old age, if called upon. In Karadehti Tiaso, she also had a sword sister who could charm the sun itself if she wanted. In all the years Nydera knew her, she didn't know Karadehti to enjoy sweating unless it involved a sword in her hand or a man or two, or ten, in her bed. Heat was something Olmarians were born into. Their people had survived thousands of years under its strength. None of that made days like today easier. Which was why they had walked out of the village, starting south of the Bed of Petals, past the grove, to walk the trench project. If the Bound Boys had to work in these conditions, the least their Paramount could do was step out under the blazing sun and be seen among them.

"The desert never yields," Nydera reminded her best friend and trusted advisor.

"The desert never yields."

Karadehti had her hair pulled up into a tight bun, the traditional Olmarian fighting style, the Warrior's Embrace. Today, like many women around the village, Karadehti wore her hair in the embrace because of the heat, not battle. Olma-Ka hadn't seen a battle in its lands since Nydera became Paramount. Long may that last for the settled Sun Skinned people. Even now that she'd made aggressive moves. After all, regardless of how many elders complained or people whispered at the bathing pool about the disgrace they felt at the new defensive structure going up, that was why she was leading the stockade project. No recent invasions didn't mean they'd never come again. They would. Just in which form?

They had Taowen Isock, the rich merchant from Hastelle, imprisoned. Three of her most trusted warriors were in the Dark Sands searching for the Crown of Spikes. Everything was going in the right direction. They were solidifying their hold on this region of the Olka-Fa as the vanguard of all Sun Skinned. The fields were expanding as the engineers taught the farmers irrigation. Their defenses were improving daily so, should favor turn against them, Olmarians would have a better chance to defend all they'd earned.

The trench was only the first phase of defense, and the project was progressing nicely, all things considered.

Nydera wore a proud smile as they continued west, not for the benefit of the incredible young men who tore away at the desert, but because their dedication truly amazed her. Two Bound Boys scrambled to find their shovels when they saw her coming. Wearing scowls, most likely aimed at her, they resumed their work nonetheless. Problems. A Paramount always had them. The trench stretched alongside their path, running out toward the planting fields. When it curved to the north, Nydera embraced the accomplishment. The Bound Boys, under the supervision of the toughest Freed women, those who knew how to treat the young men humanely, were working through difficult conditions. Nydera saw how it taxed them—a necessary sacrifice. Once the trench was complete, the construction of the stockade would begin. Until then, they would be open for invasion, especially from the Buk Toh of Hastelle. The Merchant Mercenaries wouldn't rest as long as Taowen Isock was in Olmarian hands. As much as she disliked pushing the Bound Boys so hard, their work and sacrifices were for the greater good. They were blood in the sand.

"The project looks great," Karadehti said, breaking Nydera's reflection. "You must be pleased?"

"I am," Nydera said softly, glancing toward the south.

"Doesn't sound like it." Karadehti snickered.

"I *am*."

With a hand around her wrist, Karadehti pulled her to a stop before gently but firmly spinning her. "Nydera, you may be the Paramount, but I will kick your ass right here if you are not honest. Fortunately for you, the work crews aren't close enough to witness your demise, so at least your honor will remain after I'm done with you."

Standing for a silent moment, Nydera was the first to crack, breaking out in laughter. A spring of hair fell when she tipped her head, and she brushed it back.

"This project is not easy on them," Nydera admitted. "I worry about their health and how much longer they can work at this rate."

"They're Olmarian. Proud Bound Boys," Karadehti said. "More importantly, they're blood in the sand. You know that. They will do their duty. If that means digging deep trenches, they will dig the biggest, widest, deepest ditch in the Olka-Fa, and they'll do it without complaint. What are you truly worried about?"

Karadehti was correct. What did worry her? As Olmarians, their honor was their loyalty. These young men would do what was asked of them, as all Olmarians did. Some might complain, but they'd do so out of earshot of her, the elders, and the Freed. Most wouldn't. They'd work as hard on this as they would earning their Mark on the next raid. Still, this project signaled a marked shift in not only Olmarian thinking, but in their culture. Convincing the village elders to invest in this project had been hard enough. Too many nights spent in disagreement over this undertaking. Resolution was slow in visiting their people. Some saw it as wasteful, and that was difficult enough for her to deal with. But it was those who saw it as cowardly who had forced Nydera's hand to become the arbiter she didn't want to be.

The old ways cannot become the new. Lately, she'd had to remind herself of that principle too often.

Those voices had quieted once Nydera forced them to see her way, uncomfortable as it was to do so. But she hadn't silenced them, either. In the end, the elders supported her. But if they struggled to accept this new way of life, how would those who didn't have access to her thinking feel about this shift? None of the Freed women she tasked to supervise reported anything troubling, even from the Bound Boys who sweated under the sun for endless days. Nydera knew, though, just because she wasn't hearing the complaints didn't mean whispers didn't carry them to every tent in the village. She was asking Olmarians to lose a bit who they were, of what defined the proud Sun Skinned. That was not a simple request, and it would be reckless not to think on it often.

"Doing the right thing for my people," Nydera answered finally, softly.

Karadehti was closer, running a soft hand up Nydera's arm, sending shivers through the Paramount. Karadehti's touch felt like the rare times Nydera had seen a black sky pierced by lightning. Enticing. Karadehti could seduce the twin moons—the cold, lonely and lost companions of the sun.

Her full brown eyes softened. "You are doing what you think is best for Olma-Ka. No one can fault you for that."

Nydera held back the anguish barreling down on her as the memories of the criticisms from the elders flooded back. She nudged her chin at the closest work crew. "But not what is best for them."

Karadehti's forehead wrinkled.

Seeing that she'd confused her friend, Nydera clarified. "You said that I'm doing what I think is best."

"You are."

"Exactly." Nydera took a slow breath. "I trust you more than anyone, Karadehti. I need you to speak frankly. Is this project the insane idea of an untethered Paramount?"

Karadehti turned to take in the long stretch of desert ripped open by Olmarian shovels. "People will always struggle to understand geniuses."

Nydera barked a hoarse, bitter laugh.

Karadehti's thick eyebrows turned down. "You asked for my thoughts, sword sister, and I'm not about to mislead you now. You see things differently than others. Sure, you have seen other parts of the world, places every other Olmarian will die before seeing. That has helped you consider grand plans, but that is not your only gift. The way you think, how you're able to anticipate twists, plan for them before anyone else even sees the possibilities or threats. Those types of things don't sit right with simpler types. That is not a slight. It's the truth. A truth you must learn to deal with and stop questioning. Your concern shouldn't be what Olmarians think of your ideas." Karadehti stopped, squinting. "Do you know how to tell if you're insane or not?"

The question drew an ugly cry-laugh from Nydera. "No. How?"

Karadehti moved closer again, rubbing Nydera's arm, sending tingles up her skin and raising bumps that didn't go without notice. Her sword sister smiled coyly. "When you are on your deathbed and the people who question you now are still alive to question you then. That's how you'll know you were never insane, but the Paramount Olma-Ka needed at these times."

"We still don't know. I could have brought home the struggle, right to their tents," Nydera said.

"How so?"

"By taking the merchant."

"He is indebted to us," Karadehti said, her voice full of heat. "He should be grateful you didn't have his throat slit."

"It would be hard for him to repay a debt that way," Nydera said with a frustrated sigh. "I don't know, sister. By doing this, I have invited the hostility of those concerned with his business. The Hastelli will react."

"Let them come," Karadehti said with a shrug. "We will deal with them if they do. Isn't that part of the reason you're having this built? It will only help us. See? You're a genius in action. Steps ahead of even the sharpest Olmarian."

Nydera bit down on her lip. "Let's see if you still feel that way when the Steelborn stand on the other side of this trench."

Karadehti laughed. "They'll cook inside their steel plates under the sun long before they reach Olma-Ka." More rubbing. More tingling. "Relax. You're doing what is best for Olma-Ka. I know that. The wise ones know that. In time, everyone will see what you're trying to accomplish here."

"Thank you, sword sister," Nydera said, hugging Karadehti. Even in the heat of the day, Karadehti smelled of fresh cloves. "Let's see how today's work has progressed, shall we? It will take my mind off the Bitter River, Steelborn, mercenaries, and the merchant."

Karadehti bounced her eyebrows. "So much fun, isn't it? Being in charge, that is. Disenfranchised villagers. The waters of the river lowering again. Needing to build defenses to keep out hostile peoples. Have I told you I don't envy you?"

The pair shared a laugh as they made their way to the spot where most of the crew was working today. Bound Boys spread along the northern reach now approaching the northwest guard tower.

"Impressive," Karadehti observed.

Nydera had to agree. The crew was making excellent progress. However, one short analysis hinted at a group who weren't working as hard as the rest. She squinted against the shimmering heat waves. "Who are they?"

Her sword sister shielded her eyes. "Too far away. Let's get a little closer and see who these lazy bastards are."

Moving along the trench, Nydera and Karadehti took time to move toward the small group, stopping occasionally to talk to those who labored. They looked ragged. More than one shot side-long glances at them as they passed. Not the affectionate exchanges of the past, before her decree to wall the village off from the desert. Nydera wondered how tired they truly were, since each seemed to try to hide their state when they noticed her watching. She kept a firm expression and a light voice to encourage and empower them, to help them own their part in strengthening the village. Most of the Bound Boys were in good spirits, laughs, chatter, and some songs filling the long hole in the desert. She felt encouraged that the negative comments by the elders hadn't reached the ears of the Bound. At least, not yet. When they approached the group standing to the side, still not contributing to the project, her mood changed.

"Stop here," she said, grabbing Karadehti's firm arm. "Look. What do you see?"

Karadehti examined the boys. "Bound Boys."

"And?"

Nydera's sword sister shrugged, nonplussed. "Nevilan. Are you shocked he isn't doing what he's supposed to be? I'm pretty sure he believes himself allergic to labor."

The comment was meant to be humorous, but Nydera

wasn't in a laughing mood anymore. She'd given the Two–Marked man responsibility for this portion of the project. He was a Freed man and completely under-utilized because she couldn't trust him. When Heliran Andel, Nevilan and Gaeron's mother, had died, Nydera promised to be an extended guardian for the boys. She was the Paramount, and couldn't give them the attention of a mother in their real mother's absence, but she'd done as much as she could. Over the sun cycles, she'd learned just how intolerable Nevilan could be. At first, she attributed that to his mother's death. In time, she learned that was his unwavering nature. Nothing more.

The task should have been straightforward. Yet, the first time she checked in on him, he was not only not assisting, but pulling others away from their tasks.

"What do you think he's plotting?" she asked. "Because, that does not look innocent."

"Nevilan? There's no telling," Karadehti said with an exasperated breath.

"That's the problem, isn't it?"

"I told you my fear about the wrong brother coming back from the raid in Hastelle," Karadehti said with a chuckle. "While I'm glad Gaeron returned, that relief was balanced by the fact that Nevilan did."

Nydera agreed but wouldn't put voice to it. Not that she didn't trust Karadehti. She didn't want anyone accidentally overhearing. Such a sentiment was beneath a Paramount. All Olmarians were her people, even the type who made her want to sleep with her eyes open—the ones like Nevilan Andel. Still, the shame was there, seething under her skin. She had hoped the gods would deliver a kind fate by having tragedy introduce itself to Nevilan on the raid of the city to abduct Taowen Isock. The gods hadn't listened.

"I don't know how else to deal with him," Nydera admitted as they crept forward. She didn't want to stray too close, didn't want him aware she was observing him. Right now, he was so engrossed in his conversation with the Bound Boys, he hadn't noticed. But he may. Nevilan was no fool. "Every task I give him, he somehow finds a way to cause me troubles."

"You think that huddle spells trouble?"

"I don't want to think it does," Nydera answered honestly. "But, this is Nevilan."

"I wouldn't put it past him."

"Nor I."

Nevilan dropped his head, his shoulders rocked. Thoughts raced through her mind, and she tried to stop them before she got carried away. It was enough to be paranoid about Chali and her ambitions. Nydera didn't have the energy to add a second name to the list. Yet, if anyone's name topped that list, it would be the man she watched.

Karadehti harrumphed. "You know, where the Hastelli failed, I can help you?" She wiggled her eyebrows.

Nydera couldn't not laugh, even though it darkened her thoughts. "Please, enlighten me."

"The way I see it, he should have fallen in Hastelle." Karadehti raised her bottom lip, which forced the corners of her mouth down as if she were contemplating life's greatest mysteries. "But he didn't. Where the Hastelli couldn't get the job done, I can. With your permission, of course."

"Oh yeah? How, exactly, would you do that?"

Karadehti dipped her head, mouth now forming a line. "Well, he is a Freed man, is he not?"

"He is."

"Then I could take him to the Bed of Petals."

"And how would that help solve this problem?"

"Nydera. Nydera. Nydera," Karadehti said as if she were speaking to a child. "Simple, sweet, sword sister. I would fuck him until his heart explodes."

"Somehow, I imagine you would enjoy that for a multitude of reasons." As an afterthought, she added, "Even if it was Nevilan you laid with."

"Oh, I would. Trust me," Karadehti said. Something flickered across her face. Before Nydera could ask, Karadehti's tone dropped, her voice losing its humor. "I would bed that entire group if it would help you. And maybe one of those bastards has strong enough seed to finally give me offspring."

There it was. The truth. The greatest tragedy Aabiku, the god of fertility and sexuality, bestowed upon anyone. Her sword sister, the most trusted advisor, a warrior, Karadehti would never realize the true elevated station of a Freed woman until she bore a child. It was not the Olmarian way. It was the old way, but beliefs were slow to change. Bound Boys, women having "the flaw" if their bodies were too slim, lower honor secretly bestowed on Freed who didn't produce children. The thinking of a culture that would be left to the ravages of time if they didn't change. Regardless of how hard she worked to change that mentality, she could not force new ways. In the eyes of all the Freed who were brazen or ignorant enough to admit it, Karadehti was lesser Freed because she had not yet had a child.

A bitter fact of Olmarian life.

Children were a great gift from the gods, but the impact bearing them had on a woman's reputation was embarrassing, if she was honest. Karadehti was not lesser because she'd never been a mother. Yet, that was an unwavering truth for too many of the Freed women who silently questioned her right to stand at Nydera's side.

What do they think of me in silence?

Her child, Umtu, was killed while on an expedition to the Trident when the squad Nydera led was ambushed by bandits. Having lost him was likely harder than never having one to lose, but she would never say such a thing to her sword sister.

"If I'm not allowed to ridicule myself, then you aren't

either," the Paramount said, wrapping an arm around Karadehti's shoulder and pulling her close. "You are very much every part of a Freed woman as anyone in the village."

Karadehti leaned her head on Nydera's shoulder. "Even Osla?"

Nydera nodded even though her best friend couldn't see it. "Even Osla."

"She has eight children," Karadehti said as if a reminder was needed.

"Our food stores are very aware of that fact," Nydera said with a chuckle. "And she isn't half the warrior you are."

"There are many who would disagree with you."

Nydera pulled away, grabbed Karadehti by the shoulders and turned her so she could remind the most important woman in her life of her earlier message. "If I'm half the Paramount you think I am, they will live long lives and be able to remind me on my deathbed that they disagree with me."

The twinkle returned to Karadehti's eyes. "You're not allowed to use my reasoning against me."

"I think I just did."

"Unfair."

Nydera tugged, marching Karadehti toward the small group as she glanced down at her sword sister's red robe that exposed far too much cleavage. "Let's see if we can motivate Nevilan to get to work… without having to show off your tits."

"You're a Paramount, not a god. And I happen to think my tits are glorious. Why not show them off?"

They didn't get the chance. Before they reached the cluster, Leonaime Nynar, a rotund elder Freed woman who most in Olma-Ka held in high esteem, stomped toward Nevilan with her thick arms swinging in high arcs. "Get to work! Get to work! Now, boys! Get to work!"

Karadehti chuckled. "Think we should get involved?"

Nydera shot her a look of disbelief. "With Leonaime? Are

you crazy? Even I wouldn't combat that woman. She would tear me apart with her words alone."

Karadehti nodded. "Very wise decision. This is why you are the Paramount. I prefer to stay as far away from Leonaime as I can when she's in these moods."

Nevilan, instead of returning Leonaime's wild movements, clasped his hands in front of him, lifting his chin with an air of superiority. "Do not speak to me in such a way, Leonaime. I am Two–Marked."

"I am very aware of your status," Leonaime said, pushing out her broad chest.

Nydera noted Leonaime didn't mention Nevilan's status as being earned.

"I'm in charge of this work detail," Nevilan said.

Leonaime lifted a single finger to the air, shoulder height. "And I am in charge of overseeing the entire project, Nevilan. You've dawdled long enough. I won't tell you again. Get back to work. All of you."

Nevilan's hands dropped. Karadehti mumbled an insult and took a step forward.

Nydera grabbed her arm. "No, don't interrupt."

Karadehti shot her a confused look.

"You'll insult Leonaime," Nydera said. "She can handle this. If that changes, I'll set you loose on our newest Two-Marked."

"Promise?"

Nydera nodded, never taking her eyes off Nevilan. Even though his long black hair, its tan highlights brought out in the bright day, blocked his bearded face, Nydera could sense his sneer. "I promise."

"These men will return to work when I say they return," Nevilan shouted, emphasizing the new and public status of his small group. "And if you ever—" Nevilan cut off as he glanced to his side and noticed the Paramount. He straightened, taking a long moment to adjust his red robe, leaning toward Leonaime and speaking so lowly only the pair of them shared the message.

Then he swung around to the small group of men. Nydera couldn't hear what he said, but they snatched their shovels and jumped into the trench as if the sand they lingered on had suddenly burned.

Nevilan's narrow frame drifted to the edge of the ditch, away from Leonaime who supervised from farther up the slope. She crossed her arms and watched. She tipped her chin up slightly, the sun catching the thin band of her grey in her hairline.

Karadehti whistled. "You've got your hands full with that one. Have I ever told you that I don't envy you?"

"Numerous times," Nydera said. "Let's just hope Gaeron returns soon from the Dark Sands."

"Why?"

"I wouldn't want to have to explain to him why I killed Nevilan while he was on a mission."

5

NEVILAN

WHEN THE SUN FINALLY SLEPT, the air took a chill. The black night sparkled with twinkling points of light. Nevilan sat on the driftwood bench that had been a gift to his parents a generation ago. Pulled from the Sweet Waters River, a craftsman his mother had rescued from a babite had repaid his debt by burning a hunting scene into the wood with a hot iron. The bench always received compliments, even all these sun cycles later. But Nevilan didn't care. A bench was a bench. A mead skin dangled between his knees as he hunched forward.

Creatures skittered underneath the sand anytime someone walked one of the pathways, most heading to the Circle of Fire where most Olmarian social activities took place. He would not be joining the fires tonight. The day's events bothered him.

What had started out so promisingly ended when the old bitch Leonaime Nynar interfered with his gathering of Bound Boys. Under other circumstances, she wouldn't have been a problem. Nevilan was too aware of his surroundings to fall into hidden traps. Nydera and her cunt best friend were watching Leonaime confront him, but he had foiled their plans to embarrass him and strip him of honor in front of those he hoped to influence. Their ploy had come as a surprise but had failed. Rash reactions would not have served him. Nevilan was pleased that he kept his cool in the face of hostility from three Freed women.

But those troubles still seethed in his gut. Under better conditions he would have retreated to the interior of his tent, where he could ponder his next steps. As it was, the tent was stifling, and would offer no reprieve for his busy mind. Still so much to plan. And now he needed to add the Paramount and her small circle of trusted advisors to his thoughts. Why hadn't he expected this? Of course, they would see him as a threat. He should have been ready. But he wasn't.

No matter now. He swirled the mead in a tight circle. *I'm ready now. The opportunity isn't lost.*

"Nevilan?" the quiet voice interrupted.

Rercan approached tentatively. The shorter man with rich brown skin and hooked nose took timid steps. Nevilan held his internal groan. "What do you want?"

Rercan looked taken aback. "Would you—would you like company?"

Nevilan wouldn't, but he slid sideways on the bench, making room. Company might do well to pull him out of his temper. The anger building was interfering with his thinking. It wasn't helpful—a distraction to his larger goal. He couldn't be influenced by its toxicity. Clear thinking came with calm. If Rercan served no other purpose, he could help achieve that.

"Thank you," Rercan said as he sat. "Are you... are you okay? You seem troubled."

"I am," Nevilan replied, staring at the mead skin before offering it to Rercan.

The hook-nosed Bound Boy raised his skin. "I brought one. I thought you might want a drink. Seems like we were thinking the same thing." His laugh wavered.

Nevilan found no humor in the situation. The fat old bitch

interrupted him when he had the Bound Boys hanging on his every word. He had been about to deliver a hammer to the anvil, to open their eyes to the possibilities. She would pay for that, but later. The timing had to be right. Now, he had to construct a situation where he could get them alone, unwatched, and finish delivering his message.

The drink went a long way in helping him release the day's aggravation. He was glad to see Rercan thinking along the same lines, something else that distinguished his friend from Tocan.

"Yes, I plan on drinking a lot of mead tonight," Nevilan said.

Moments passed. A few tents away, a woman groaned in ecstasy, loudly, as if she were bragging to the entire village about getting her fill of cock. It reminded Nevilan that he had not tasted a woman since the night of his Freeing ceremony. Rercan had hired a whore when none of the other Freed women expressed interest. One day, each one who had rejected him would regret that decision. But they were insignificant, at least until his time came.

"Those things you said earlier today, at the ditch... did you mean them?" Rercan asked timidly.

Slowly, Nevilan turned, indulging himself in making the shorter man squirm in the silence.

Rercan looked away. "I... I ask because they... we, I mean... we talked about it throughout the day. I think they really understood what you're saying. I think you got them thinking about it... about what you said. About the situation. About the unfairness. But I think they're scared as well."

"Scared of what?"

Rercan lifted his pointy chin, looking toward the Circle of Fire. The faint orange light flickered on his face, his large nose casting wide shadows. "Of what we are, Nevilan. Olmarians aren't scared by anything, at least that's what everyone says. But we do fear. That's the truth of it."

"Like what?" Nevilan had his ideas of what Olmarians feared, especially the Bound Boys, even many Freed men. They fear the women. They always had. Women dominated them, always holding positions of authority and speaking with impunity. Olmarian men were cowards. Vicious with onyx or steel in their hands, their minds were feeble, almost infantile.

"Like... like those things you mentioned," Rercan said. "There's a difference between understanding and agreeing with what you said, and being able... being courageous enough to act. They'll never stand up for themselves, Nevilan. Those who are smart enough are too weak. Those strong enough are too dumb."

"Then we need to help them," Nevilan said, taking a long swig of his mead.

"How?"

"By helping them see the possibilities."

Rercan cleared his throat. "These men aren't as intelligent as you. They don't understand talk like that. They need simple ideals, things they can imagine, see in their own minds. If you want them to understand your perspective, if you want them to grasp what you're trying to teach, help them see that."

"How do you propose I do that?"

"Start by explaining what you want for yourself."

"What I want for myself? I'll tell you exactly what I want. I want to be the most powerful Freed man in Olma-Ka. No. I want to be more than that. I want to be the first-ever male Paramount of Olma-Ka."

Rercan looked around nervously. When he spoke, his voice was low, holding a nervousness he tried to hide. "You can't speak such things."

"Why not?"

Rercan fidgeted on the driftwood bench, fingering his mead skin. His head swiveled, constantly checking the path, and then again ahead, as if he expected the current Paramount to appear from around every corner. "We have a Paramount."

Nevilan shrugged, trying to convey the confidence he felt. The mead emboldened his actions. "No Paramount is permanent. Their claim can be challenged at any time."

"Yes, by other Freed women," Rercan said, emphasizing the last word. "You are Two–Marked, but you're still a man. We have no claim to the Paramount."

"And why is that?" he asked. When Rercan didn't answer, Nevilan knew, no matter how much he trusted his friend, Rercan could never be half the visionary he was. Therefore, the other man could never be fully trusted. A disappointing limitation. But none of the crew he was trying to groom were different. They didn't have a leader who was strong enough to help them imagine the possible. A strong leader, like a male Paramount. "When Nydera challenged Sariona Petrosiana, she claimed the old ways would not become the new. Yet here we are, nearly two decades into her reign, and how much has changed? Truly? Sure, we are building physical defenses for the village, but that's because we are growing cowardly. How much else has changed?"

Rercan gave his head a shake. His bangs, almost as long as the hair on the side of his head, flopped over his eyes. With a toss of his head, he brushed them aside. "Change is slow. She involves Freed men in how we're governed more often. The stories say no other Paramount has had so many Freed men serve as elders throughout a claim."

"Platitudes. Empty gestures to please stupid people. Nothing more," Nevilan spat, drawing a deep breath and calming his agitated nerves. He offered his mead to Rercan. "Drink mine. It's a delightful blend. I think you might enjoy it."

Rercan took the skin, his eyes on Nevilan. When he drank, his eyes widened in surprise. The wine Nevilan had taken from one of the root cellars pleased his hook-nosed friend. Only the Freed had access to the cellars and had an agreement they would only take their fair portion. Nevilan had taken three skins. Rightfully. Who had done more than him for Olmarians? Especially over the past few moon cycles? No one. Three skins of wine was hardly fair compensation. This was his deserved reward, one he shared with Rercan now for a purpose.

"That's good," Rercan said, smacking his lips and looking reluctant when he pulled the skin away from his mouth. "Where did you get it?"

Nevilan took the skin back, emptying a healthy quantity before answering. "From the stores. The one reserved for us Freed. It's so full, Rercan. So full. Why wouldn't it be? There are so few Freed men, of course. We can't consume as much as the Bound and the children."

"Everyone knows about them, but I didn't realize the Freed enjoy so much more. I didn't realize the cellars held so much wine that anyone could take more than they could consume."

"Not anyone. The Freed." Nevilan rolled his lips. "The mead is better. The grains are fresher. The meats are not only salted, but they're seasoned and hold much longer. Free of vermin, too. And wine, of course. We have so much of it. Life as a Freed is much, much better than a Bound. You really have no idea until your band has been broken. Such a glorious benefit."

Rercan dropped his head and stared at his mead.

Nevilan held the grin which insisted on spreading. He had his friend thinking, entertaining forbidden thoughts. "So when you tell me I can't say things like that, that I can't talk about being the first male Paramount, I want you to think about why you think along those lines in the first place. Why do you react like that? Why do you regurgitate the lessons they have taught you since you were a child? Why do any of us, Rercan? I'm not chastising you. I'm asking you to think."

"It's heresy to say such things," Rercan said weakly, unable to meet Nevilan's eyes.

"Says who?"

Rercan opened his mouth to answer, cocking his head. He snapped his mouth shut. Now Nevilan allowed his grin to take full form.

In the distance, the sweet melody of a lute filled the air. A round of cheering rose along with it. "You talk about the men not understanding my message. Though I wish I could make things better for them, I can't do it alone. I need help. They need a strong leader to see the possibilities, but a strong leader does not rise into such a position through force alone. They must have support. I need support. I need you. You can help me communicate my message to those who need to hear it."

The music from the Circle of Fire grew louder. Songs filled the night sky.

"Simple people need simple things. That much is true. When they have them, they are satiated, hungering for nothing more. That is the true danger." Nevilan paused, pointedly looking toward the source of music. His attention was on his periphery, where Rercan watched him.

After a moment Rercan asked, "Mead and music? That's what you mean?"

Nevilan gave his friend a reassuring smile, reaching over and placing a hand on his shoulder. "See? You get it. Provide just enough mead, just enough food, and just enough free time filled with entertainment, and a population becomes docile. Comfort is the enemy of progress. They stop thinking about how much more they could have, about how much better things could be. This doesn't have to be a game of competition, where only the elite have access to the better mead. To wine." Between them, he held aloft his skin filled with the expensive wine while dipping his head at Rercan's mead, marking the divide. "It doesn't have to be this way."

Nevilan swirled the wine. Not that it needed it, but for show. The skin was almost empty. He placed it at his lips and swallowed the rest of the sweet blend. When he finished, he smacked his lips. "Every man in this village should understand the pleasure of sweet wine after a long, hot day."

Rercan didn't answer, which was best. Nevilan didn't want him talking. He wanted him wondering, pondering. He wanted Rercan and the other men to be forming questions to which they already had answers. Answers they feared to recognize. Answers he would provide instead.

"How can I help?" Rercan asked after a quiet moment.

"Come with me."

Nevilan stood, tossing the empty skin on the bench. Rercan followed. They took the long way through the organized rows of tents, avoiding the night's festivities in the Circle of Fire.

One of the benefits of an evening that followed such a miserably hot day was that the heat took its toll on his people. Those who weren't drinking and singing near the circle were in their tents. Many of the Freed fucked, their grunts and groans low under the lute. The Bound, unable to pursue pleasures of the flesh, chatted by candlelight inside their homes. Many more slept.

Nevilan and Rercan crossed Olma-Ka without drawing attention. As a Two-Marked, he could do anything he wanted, but old habits were hard to break. He'd still readied his explanation in case a Freed woman inquired about their activities, an explanation that would now go unused.

They cleared the last row of tents, and Nevilan continued toward the edge of the village, where tents gave way to open land and the last building to define the boundaries of Olma-Ka. The stables. He lost the outline of the largest building in the village against the backdrop of the night.

"Are we going to see him?" Rercan asked in a tight voice.

In the darkness, Nevilan smiled at his friend's intuition.

Past the tents, a solitary structure stood apart. A few hundred yards shy of the stables, the large cage stood away from tents, the Circle of Fire, or anything else. The nearest structure was the northeast watchtower, and that was still a safe distance away. Close enough for an adept bowwoman to keep prisoners in line, the watchtower was too far away for whoever manned it to make out the visitors to the cage, especially a night-time visit. With bars of blackened steel as thick as a normal man's arms, there was no breaking them. The roof, a solid structure coated in black pitch that soaked in the sun's power during the day, was expansive but stopped just beyond the cage's frame. The cage had no use for shade. Prisoners liked shade, sought it out in the hottest parts of the day. The cage was designed to break, not to provide comfort.

Before the cage, a solitary guard stood over a small fire flickering in the open terrain against the desert wind.

He was tall, half a foot beyond six feet. His naked arms exposed carved muscle. The guard's mass of curly black hair fell to mid-chest. Nevilan couldn't remember his name. The guard watched them with more curiosity than prudence.

"I will speak to the prisoner," Nevilan said forcefully when they approached.

The guard's expression was flat. "Okay."

Torches circled the cage, casting weak light from all sides. However, the flickering flame didn't reach the middle. In that murkiness, the prisoner sat, his knees pulled up to his chest, his arms wrapped around them, and his head dropped behind his arms.

"Taowen Isock, I will speak with you," Nevilan said, sticking his chest out farther.

The Buk Toh's hair was disheveled from his short imprisonment. Sun cycles ago it may have been a very light brown, a color rarely seen in Olma-Ka but probably common in

Hastelle. The years had washed all but the most determined vibrancy from Isock's hair.

The head behind the arms didn't move.

"Maybe he's asleep?" Rercan whispered.

Nevilan doubted that. The prisoner was in enemy hands, his nearest allies and friends a hundred miles to the south. He wasn't sleeping; he was avoiding interacting with those who thought to harm him. Rercan missed that. Nevilan didn't want to draw the guard's attention.

The prisoner answered Rercan's dilemma in a smooth, foreign tongue. "I am not sleeping. I'm thinking."

"Thinking about what?" Rercan asked.

The prisoner lifted his head. The man's nose dominated his face, bulbous and shaped like a pear. The skin around his eyes was wrinkled from many sun cycles of life. His crystal eyes, the color of the sky on the brightest days, defied his age with their effervescence. "Those are thoughts I do not wish to share with my captors."

"We're not your captors," Nevilan said.

The prisoner straightened. "Are you not? You are Sun Skinned."

"But it was not our choice to imprison you."

"Then set me free," Taowen said, his expression as flat as the guard's had been.

Nevilan gave the man a smile. It was returned. Neither was friendly. "We both know I cannot do that."

The prisoner nodded. "I figured as much. So why are you interrupting my contemplations?"

Nevilan spoke as he slowly circled the cage, moving to the far side, away from the guard. Taowen watched the pair, adjusting to not lose sight of them. "I was hoping to have a conversation with you."

"About?" Taowen asked.

"I'm curious what you have to offer that has put you in your current situation."

"This situation was not my choice. I am not here of my own volition. You would have to ask your Paramount why I sit behind these bars."

"I'd rather ask you."

"Aye. I can see that." Taowen pulled his arms off his bent knees, which dropped to his sides, spreading apart. Then he lifted his arms horizontally, palms up. "But I don't see how answering you will benefit me. You have already taken part of my night, and yet I still sit behind these bars. That doesn't seem like a fair trade since only one of us benefits."

Nevilan cursed himself for not considering bringing a token of goodwill to the abducted merchant. He swatted Rercan's arm with the back of his hand. "Give him your mead."

"Are you sure?"

"Do it."

Rercan untied his skin and tossed it into the cage. The skin hit the sand near the merchant's slippered feet. Like the man's cloak, the slippers were purple and appeared to be soft felt, hardly practical footwear for the desert.

Taowen didn't move. He looked at the skin and then at the pair. "How do I know that isn't poison?"

"What reason do I have to poison you? Neither of us benefit from that."

Taowen squinted. He reached for the skin, lifting it and pulling the cork. Without a word, he put it to his lips and sucked at the skin, wiping his lips with the back of his hand when he finished. He held up the skin for inspection. "That has to be the worst mead I've ever had, but by the gods, does it taste good. Thank you."

"You're welcome. Thank you for trusting me."

"I imagine it would have dishonored you to kill me with poison," Taowen said, his narrowed eyes firmly on Nevilan now, Rercan all but ignored. "After all, that isn't the Olmarian way, is it? Your kind much prefer your bloodlust to smarter uses of resources. Subversion isn't really in your nature."

"True, we are not barbarians," Nevilan said with enough venom to equal the imprisoned merchant's attitude, yet not so much as to shut down the conversation. "Killing isn't in my interest."

"What is your interest, then?" Taowen asked, raising the skin back to his lips and drinking more of Rercan's mead.

Nevilan squatted to eye-level with the prisoner. He dropped his voice. "Why did Nydera want you captured? Why imprison you?"

"Does your Paramount not share with the rest of the village? I thought you Olmarians shared everything? Information. Food. Your women… or your boys." Taowen sneered, the cracks around his mouth deepening.

Nevilan would not bite on the antagonistic comment. "She has not shared her interest in you. Yet we sent an army to Hastelle with the purpose of bringing you back to Olma-Ka." He waved at the cage. "And here you sit, a caged animal readied to be slaughtered. Why?"

"What do I get out of sharing?" Taowen asked.

"Is every conversation an exchange?"

At that, Taowen smirked. "I wouldn't be the richest merchant in Hastelle if it wasn't."

Interesting. Nevilan suspected the man had coin. That much was evident during the raid in Hastelle when their squad broke into his headquarters to abduct him. The building wasn't even the merchant's permanent home, yet it was filled with riches beyond those of anyone in Olma-Ka except the Paramount herself. To discover the man was wealthy was no surprise. To discover he was the richest of his kind in the large city was a pleasant one.

"What would you want?"

"Information for information," Taowen said. "If you want to know my story, I want to know yours."

"My story? Why?"

"Call me curious," Taowen said. "As long as I've been here, the only people who visit are those bringing food. My guess is that your Paramount very much wants me to remain alive. I find it strange that I haven't even seen her yet."

"Nydera hasn't come to see you?"

Taowen cocked his head, squinting. "You call her by her name."

"I do. What of it?"

"My experience with your culture backs up my understanding of it. Olmarians place great value on their Paramount. In fact, at least the way we understand it, there have been Paramounts who have been deified. To hear you use her name is interesting, to say the least."

"She's human, just like the rest of us," Nevilan said confidently, feeling the truth of every word boil inside him. "Just as she calls me by my name, I call her by hers."

"And what is yours?"

"Nevilan."

Taowen dipped his head. The disheveled spikes of brown and gray hair tipped. He didn't bother to fix what fell out of place. "A pleasure, Nevilan. I am Taowen Isock, merchant of Hastelle. At this point in my life, Merchant's Row is essentially my kingdom. Not bad for a kid born into poverty, I'd say. Quite the rise to everyone who watched my journey. Especially those who attempted to interfere with it. But, pfffaw, most of them either live in squalor now or are dead. I made sure of that. What's your story?"

"Not nearly as rich as yours, in many ways. Let's just say I am an Olmarian born to the wrong people, at the wrong time, wanting the wrong things."

A dangerous twinkle flashed in Taowen's eyes. For a moment, Nevilan criticized himself for this approach. Maybe it was too soon. Too risky until he had more say, more leverage. He felt completely outmatched by the merchant.

"What is it you want, Nevilan? Maybe I can help you obtain it. That is my business, after all."

"There are many things I want."

If his ambiguity bothered Taowen, the prisoner didn't let it show. Instead, he sat slightly straight, adjusting his rich purple cloak, embroidered with a design of apothecary scales. "Let's start with what you want at this moment."

They were feeling each other out. Slowly building trust. The merchant was absorbing the unspoken messages Nevilan sent.

"Like I said, I want to know why she is so interested in you." He had to offer more. The merchant was the type of man who expected grand gestures, Nevilan figured. "For all the reasons you Buk Toh have for disliking us, one of the greatest attributes Olmarians possess is that we value our people. We would never put another of our kind at risk without great reason." Rercan shifted, but Nevilan ignored him. "For Nydera to send an entire squad into a hostile city to retrieve you, she must have had good justification."

"I can't say I was surprised when those barbarians broke into my headquarters, killing a number of my best men," Taowen said. "I have to admit, I underestimated your Paramount. That is my own fault, a mistake I will never repeat, should I live to see the outside of this cage."

"We believe a death in battle is an honorable one. The men you lost will be remembered honorably."

"The men I lost are dead. They don't care how they are remembered," Taowen said, his voice hotter. "Too many trusted lieutenants and business partners, though many of the others were nothing more than bodyguards. And now I will need to replace them if I am to assert my authority along Merchant's Row again." The merchant lifted a hand and pointed at the top of the cage. "If I ever get out of here. You ask what I did to gain your Paramount's attention such that she would risk losing her people to abduct me. The fact is she hides many things from you. Not only my true nature, but her own business dealings. That is why she had me abducted and has imprisoned me."

Rercan's face scrunched. Nevilan scowled. Taowen's answer fell short of satisfactory. Large pieces had been left out. Intentionally, most likely.

"What business did she have with you?"

Taowen sniffed. "For years, your Paramount has delivered a gracious amount of Olmarian goods. Items made here in the village. Crafts. Weapons. The nonperishable creations of your people. Our understanding was that I would resell those goods for her because I can negotiate greater profit margins for my friends."

"You were friends with the Paramount?" Rercan asked.

Taowen blinked, shrugging. "Not friends. I don't mix pleasure with business, and we were more like business partners."

"What went wrong?"

The wrinkled skin in the corner of Taowen's eyes curled up as he grinned. "Let's just say that my profit margins were higher than Nydera knew."

"And she found out you were robbing her? Robbing us?" Nevilan concluded.

"That is such an unfair, loaded term," Taowen said with a snicker. It was the first humor from the prisoner. "But yes, my secret was revealed by a traveling merchant who... let's just say, is a rival. The way I understand it, he was trading here and met with Nydera. That was when she discovered what I had been doing."

"So you admit to stealing from us?" Rercan asked, looking astonished. "No wonder she wanted you captured and returned. If you just pay what you owe, I'm sure she'll let you go."

"No boy," Taowen said with a sudden edge. Even his rich accent didn't soften the words. "Nydera does not plan to release me. She plans on imprisoning me, not only to work off my debt, but permanently. I won't be leaving Olma-Ka, I fear. At least, not until my spirit is freed from this realm."

There it was. An opening. "Would you give up so easily?"

"Who said I'm giving up? I'm waiting for my opportunity."

Nevilan glanced at the guard, who was too far away to hear their whispers, and didn't appear the least bit interested. "Maybe I can offer that opportunity?"

Taowen analyzed Nevilan with eyes as bright as the sky.

He felt the merchant delve deep into his soul, searching for any lack of authenticity. He would find none. Even as the silence stretched on, Nevilan refused to flinch.

"You would betray your Paramount?" Taowen finally broke his silence.

"I won't betray my people."

More silence.

"Those men your people killed were great men, but they are not the only great men aligned with me," Taowen said carefully. So carefully, Nevilan was encouraged with the direction of the conversation. "Were word to reach them of my location, they would send an armed response to free me. An action such as that would not only be appreciated, but rewarded... were someone to take up the charge."

"How would one find these men?"

Rercan gasped.

The world faded. Nevilan and Taowen locked eyes. His heart started in his chest.

"On Merchant's Row," Taowen said evenly, his eyes never leaving Nevilan. "Anyone needing to reach them would have to get into Hastelle. There, they'd have to get to the Row and ask for the Merchant Mercenaries."

"And if someone could?"

"Nevilan," Rercan whispered harshly.

Ignoring the Bound Boy, Nevilan firmed his voice. "If

someone could get to Merchant's Row. How would they find these mercenaries?"

"Carefully," Taowen said with a hint of deviousness. "Only along Merchant's Row, away from the city guard, one would need to ask for Prosper Malnit."

"Who is he?"

"If the words you have spoken are true, he is the one man who can help you achieve what you want." Taowen's lips spread in a greedy grin.

Nevilan nodded at the gift he'd made Rercan give up. "Keep the skin. We'll bring you another one when we return. Just... hide it if anyone comes." As an afterthought, he added, "Or blame it on whoever brings your next meal. I don't care. But remember, we are the ones who gifted it. I hope you wouldn't betray that."

Taowen lifted the skin in salute, took a long drink, and turned away.

"Nevilan," Rercan said, sidling next to him as they made their way back to the tent. "This is an act of treachery. What are you doing?"

Staring straight ahead, taking longer strides even though there was nothing he could accomplish tonight, Nevilan said, "I'm changing my future, Rercan. You'll go along with it and keep my secret if you don't want to be a ditch digger for the rest of your life."

6

GAERON

"Didn't you already search there?" Chali asked, squatting to move a broken slab of gray clay.

Fine sinews of muscle cut subtle curves along her legs, disappearing into her brown boots. Gaeron watched her until Drulf elbowed him. "Let your eyes linger any longer and she'll cut them out."

Gaeron blinked, recognized what he was doing, and looked away. "I... I—"

"Don't even bother finishing that." Drulf laughed, giving a hefty shake of his head that wobbled his cheeks, and walked away to continue his search.

Gaeron wiped his forehead. The sun was high, just now beginning its descent. In every direction for hundreds upon hundreds of yards, gray chunks and slabs of rock and clay lay, a broken reminder of a broken people. The Borttel Ruins were in worse condition than any of them expected. Where a city once stood, only these broken shards remained.

No structures. Only caverns dug into the desert sands, walled with this gray. Even a few of those were broken open, exposing the black belly of the desert underneath. The stone walls exposed to the open air formed foundations and demarcated property for homes, businesses, and gathering areas of the extinct people. Black sand poured over the lips of many of these ancient structures, filling their bellies and obscuring the stories these places had to tell. How their story continued was unknown. Nothing here told of who they truly were.

Nothing but sand-covered ruins.

The Crown of Spikes, wherever it was, wasn't here. Although he had no idea what it looked like, any crown, no matter how bland, would stick out in this waste.

He kicked a small chunk of clay. It tumbled and banged over more chunks. Gaeron arched his back, sore from repeatedly bending over the past two days. He didn't want to think about how many times he had. Pointless searching. He didn't want to extend it to a third.

"This is a waste, Chali," he said, kicking a broken piece of wall, or foundation, or ceiling. Did it matter? This chunk was the size of his fist. It clunked as it rolled across the rubble, dropping over the edge of a crumbled foundation and into a room that had gone unoccupied probably since the Desert King slaughtered its occupants.

She straightened. At some point in the search, she had loosened the string of her brown leather vest. The open angle of material, usually drawn together, exposed far too much skin for Gaeron to be able to concentrate on looking for a crown, no matter how majestic. Gaeron found the nearest piece of rubble to distract him. "What would you rather do?"

He shrugged, keeping his eyes off the Chaos Bender. From the hole where he'd kicked the small chunk something thudded deep within the ground. Unnaturally loud. Maybe the earth was empty under them—an unsettling thought. The thud morphed into a rattling sound as the chunk fell. What had it struck? Would she want to explore? Could they? The slat between the carved rock and the open mouth of the desert didn't look wide enough for either him or Drulf to squeeze into, even if they wanted. "Isn't there a spell you can cast that will help find this crown?"

"You're making enough noise to wake the dead." Her face scrunched. "Do you think spells like that exist?"

"I thought maybe a divination spell of some sort." Gaeron tried to ignore the dust clogging his nose by re-tying his topknot of braided hair.

"With Chaos?" Drulf said from a dozen feet away, lifting a block of clay and examining the sand underneath. Finding nothing, he dropped the clay back in its spot.

"For one, you're working too hard if you think I can use my magic for such purposes." Chali shook her head as she analyzed the broken rock around them, most of it buried under the dead sand. "And no, there is no such spell. Even if there is, I don't know it, so I certainly couldn't use it."

"Well, that's definitely something you need to look into," Gaeron said, throwing another chunk of clay. "It would make this a lot easier."

"So would not lifting every single block," Chali countered.

"Seriously. I think we can give up on the ruins. If we head to the Black Palace now, we could start our search there before the sun sleeps."

"If we stop searching here, we could miss it," Chali said.

"And? Better chances over there."

"And"—she drew out the word—"if it is here, and we waste our time trekking across the Dark Sands to the Black Palace and it's not there, we won't have the provisions to come back to the ruins."

"And if we stay in these ruins much longer, we will run out of provisions before reaching the Black Palace. Don't you think it makes much more sense that the crown would be there?"

"I'm sorry, but I have to agree with Gaeron on this," Drulf piped in, nudging a small fragment away with his foot. "I don't want to head back to Olma-Ka empty–handed either, but this search is futile. The Desert King wouldn't keep his crown here."

"The stories say he died here, with his wife by his side. They say the crown was with him at the time, that he constantly wore it during the last sun cycles of his reign," Chali said, blotting a bead of sweat from the corner of her eye with a dusty knuckle. "So if this is where he died, this is where the crown will be. In his final resting spot."

"Damn the stories, Chali. We are running out of time," Gaeron said. "We've searched this over and over and found nothing. If the crown was here, we would have seen a clue at least."

"What kind of clue?"

"I don't know," Gaeron said. "Something. A container? A riser. A throne room. At this point, I'd be happy if one of these holes was a little fancier than the others."

"Why?"

"That might give us a clue that the ruler of this kingdom actually came here instead of relying on stories older than the sands of the Olka-Fa. Right now, the only thing I see is rubble upon rubble. All of it the same. All of it picked over ages ago. If there was anything of value here, it was robbed long ago. Probably by the Scorpion Riders."

"Which clan," Drulf asked with a sniff, nodding his head.

Gaeron shrugged at Chali. "Can we at least try?"

Chali turned, her hands on tempting curves of her hips. "Fine. You two will have your way." She bent and retrieved her packs, hefting them onto her slim shoulders, and started off. Over her shoulder, she said, "Just know, if I die of hunger or thirst, my ghost will haunt you for all eternity."

Gaeron shook his head as he followed.

Picking their way through the ruins was slow going. The Black Palace loomed on the horizon, feeling no closer with each step. A symmetrical monstrosity so large it should have sunk into the desert generations ago. From this distance, the size of it promised an insurmountable task if the gods weren't with them. But it was the right decision. Every sign of life had been removed from the ruins or covered by generations of sand as the desert reclaimed the ancient city. In the ruins, they would have never found the crown. As long as the walls of the palace hadn't caved to allow the desert in, they would have a chance, regardless of the enormity of the Black Palace.

"Do you have any idea where to begin once we're inside the palace?" Gaeron asked the Chaos Bender.

She pulled up. "Why? Searching the palace was your idea. I figured you knew exactly where it would be."

"Don't be an ass," Gaeron said.

Chali put a hand to her mouth. "Do you talk to all Freed women like that? Good thing you're still a Bound Boy. Language like that won't do you any favors with women once you're Freed, no matter how many desire you."

"No Freed women desire me," Gaeron said with a shake of his head, dropping it to hide the smile he felt creeping across his lips.

Behind him, Drulf said, "Oh, gods, no. Why would you tell him that? It will go to his head."

Chali closed her eyes and groaned. "I shouldn't have said anything. Yes, Gaeron, many Freed women do. Look at you." She started walking again, even as she swept a hand from his feet to his head. "That physique is unnatural. Women are going to be curious if the rest of the package is as... unnatural. They often talk about what your Freeing ceremony will be like. They've even agreed to keep the watchtowers empty if you ever stand on the platform to break your band. Many are rooting for you."

Gaeron couldn't respond. Thoughts dashed through his head, one over another, too quickly to grasp and put voice to. Heat wrapped his neck in a clammy embrace. The platform. The breaking of the band. Becoming Freed. Moments he had dreamed about for as long as he could remember. Nothing more than a precursor to the Bed of Petals to the Freed women?

Chali chortled. "You should see your face right now. I wish we'd waited to have this conversation until we were home. I shouldn't be the only Freed woman to see that expression. I'll be sure to tell my sword sisters all about it, though. It's too special to keep all to myself."

"This has got to be the most uncomfortable I've ever been," Drulf said.

"Can we change the subject?" Gaeron asked, wishing for a cool breeze to relieve him of the flushed feeling. Grateful not to be Buk Toh, where the heat of his reaction would be laid bare for the pair to see, Gaeron tried to smile. Drulf had been embarrassed before, and his pale skin always revealed his state. The Buk Toh were too obvious, the way their pale cheeks blushed the color of a setting sun. Another reason to be grateful to the gods for being born Sun Skinned.

"Sure. What would you like to talk about?" Chali offered. "Would you like to know what a Freed woman's body looks like?"

"No. I mean, yes, but... by the gods, Chali, I already know what they look like," Gaeron said too quickly.

"Oh, do you now?" Chali laughed.

"Only because he peeks into open tents at night," Drulf joked.

"You two are asses," Gaeron said. That only drew more laughter from his friends.

"Have you ever pondered why we need to be the protectors of the Sun Skinned? All the tribes and villages, I mean?" Drulf asked after the party crossed miles of black sand, heading south.

The Black Palace appeared no nearer. Gaeron didn't mind the distracting conversation. "It is our duty."

"But why?" Drulf pressed. "Have we ever thought about that?"

"Olma-Ka is the furthest–east settlement in the desert. It is the first point of contact with the Buk Toh," Chali said.

"Yes, I know that, but that doesn't provide enough of an answer," Drulf responded, shaking his head. His cheeks jiggled. "Not for me. Geographically? Yes, it makes sense. The village is furthest east. Sure, it is the first settlement any Buk Toh would ever see. But circumnavigating our village isn't impossible. Quite easy, actually. They could get around us if they were so inclined to invade other Sun Skin settlements. The Olka-Fa is immense. The eastern edge of the desert couldn't be appropriately patrolled by ten villages. We do what we can, but to be deemed the defenders of all the desert people?"

Gaeron's chest swelled with pride. Drulf was a Buk Toh, a pale skin. Not fully. His mother was a light Sun Skinned, her complexion closer to Chali's than Gaeron's own. Whereas his was the color of the tree trunks in the grove along the southern edge of the village, Chali's skin was the color of the sands. Drulf's father was Buk Toh, and his large friend had inherited every bit of that nature. With him, it was sometimes impossible to tell when the big man was ill. In the eyes of too many Olmarians, Drulf was fully Buk Toh. But in Drulf's mind, and Gaeron's eyes, he was as Olmarian as the Paramount herself. The fact he saw himself in the same vein pleased Gaeron. Drulf could have struggled with his identity. Enough people challenged him on it throughout his life, and they would continue until he was Freed. Maybe even after. That his friend freely embraced an identity as a Sun Skinned brought Gaeron a peace he couldn't bring on his own.

"It just is," Gaeron finally said. "An honor, if I'm being honest. To be the defenders of the Sun Skinned is something that was bestowed upon us because we earned it. I'm sure there were others who could have taken that title, but it was us, the Olmarians, who earned it through blood in the sand. I take pride in that."

"Impressive for a Bonebreaker," Chali teased. "And here I thought you were too simple to understand the complexities of politics and just celebrated brute force."

"I celebrate our responsibility as well, little friend," Drulf said. "But the responsibility also creates requirements of us that other villages, towns, and even the cities farther west don't have. Think. The coin and the blood we spend to maintain the freedom for all of our kind prevents us from growing. Think of how much further along our people would be if we didn't spend our limited resources on preparing for and preventing the Buk Toh from invading." Drulf smacked his hands together. "Or coming into the Olka-Fa or through the White Plains, or the Cliffs of the Morning Star to steal our resources. Resources which belong to all Sun Skinned. Our community could be even greater if we weren't the protectors. That's all I'm saying."

"But we are already great," Chali said as if that settled the argument. "It may not seem fair, but life rarely is, Drulf. Everyone has their own obligations, obligations that benefit the greater number. Our part of that larger community is to be wardens of the east. Others have the north. The west. Ol-ta has the south. Sure, they only have Axthelm to concern themselves with. The others are shielded by the Spikes. Who knows what lies far to the west, but I'm sure they have their challenges as well. We have all the Buk Toh settlements that could come from Hastelle and the east. Yes, it's an incredible responsibility. But I can think of worse things."

"As can I," Gaeron said, about to say more, but a sound drew his attention. He turned his ear to the side to get a better listen.

Chali asked, "What is it?"

Gaeron faced Chali and Drulf. "Don't you hear that?"

They listened.

Chali bit her lip. "I don't hear anything. You look unnerved."

Bloodlust coiled. "Rattling."

"Tell me it's a snake," Drulf said. "Even a big one."

Gaeron swiveled his head slowly. Rattling. More and more rattling.

Drulf swallowed. "Skinless?"

Without life of its own, the Dark Sands helped sound carry farther than it rightfully should. Why hadn't they thought about that before they made noise at the ruins? If he could hear the skeletons, it was reasonable to think they could do the same. Now they were coming. Creatures they had only escaped because of Chali's powerful spell.

He looked into the sky. The round orb of the sun was barely visible through the dark cloud. It was lower now, of course. They had searched all day and only left when the day edged toward the point when they most likely wouldn't make the Black Palace before the sun slept. New suns had passed since their run-in with the Skinless. So, were Chali's stories about the Skinless reanimating true or not? With them coming, did it matter?

"Shit," he groaned.

They shared a look.

"But... how?" Drulf said with another large swallow.

The rattling grew.

Chali squinted. "I hear it now."

The Skinless created a racket. This time, it was more than bone rattling against bone. The other sounds had sharper notes, like stone hitting stone. Gaeron knew that sound. Onyx against onyx. Steel striking something hard. He'd heard it for years, going back to his sparring sessions as a boy.

"I can't hear anything," Drulf said, his face washing paler than before.

"Stop talking," Gaeron urged, trying to pinpoint the approaching horde. The pit was to the east. This noise came from the north, from the direction of the ruins they'd left hours ago. Its volume betrayed the potential threat. If that was a new group of skeletons... The swell of rattling. How many?

"We need to go," Gaeron said, spinning and pulling the others. If they had questions, they could ask them on the run to the palace.

"What are you thinking?" Drulf asked, not bothering to tug his arm free.

"Remember when I kicked that block and Chali told me I was making enough noise to wake the dead?" Gaeron asked. "Well, now those dead are awake."

He started jogging. Chali and Drulf kept pace.

"How sure are you?" Drulf said as he puffed from exertion after only a short while.

"Sure enough to run all the way to the Black Palace if need be," Gaeron said darkly.

"I don't know if I can do that."

Still jogging, Gaeron looked over his shoulder at his friend, who was already falling behind. Past him, a cloud rose from the desert. The cloud hovered in the same area as the sound.

"Keep going," he said, skidding to a halt and waving them on toward the palace. "I'll catch up."

Peering into the cloud of dust, Gaeron saw them. A blurred wall of white in this distance, there could be no mistaking them now. Without a need to make out their far superior numbers, he turned and bolted, soon catching the pair.

"We have to sprint. Now," he shouted, stretching out his stride.

Drulf groaned, puffing forward.

Though they crossed the desert quickly, and the palace grew, it was still miles away. Overhead, the tangle of slowly undulating clouds brought no relief in the form of a breeze, nor any rains that might slow the skeletons pursuing them across this dead land.

"We have to walk too," Chali said, her voice strained as she pulled up.

Gaeron skidded to a halt, spinning. "We can't. They're gaining, even with us running. If we walk, they will overtake us sooner."

Chali's eyes widened and slid to her side, where Drulf was bent, grabbing his knees and vomiting. "And if we run the entire way, we will never make it. We have to preserve the water we do have and ourselves."

Drulf was taxed. His enormous frame was great when handling a plow or shovel, but was doing him no favors now.

Gaeron moved to his side, wrapping his hand under the larger man's armpit. "Come. We've got to keep going. I'll help."

Drulf straightened, looking as if even that took great effort. Sweat poured down his face. "Okay. Let's go."

Over the next few miles, they alternated running as long as they could and walking whenever Drulf needed a slower pace. They neared the palace, but the pursuing cloud menaced with its approach. The rattling and sharp knocks were louder.

Gaeron didn't want to admit it, but he had to let the others know what they were about to face. "They have weapons. I can hear onyx and... I think, steel."

"Skinless with weapons?" Chali said.

"Madness. All of it," Drulf puffed. "Where... do they... come... How?"

"Enough talking, more running," Chali said, lifting her chin toward their destination. "We're getting close. That's the only chance we have, so let's stay focused on that. We'll worry about the 'wheres' and 'whys' of the Skinless later."

As they neared, the Black Palace became the horizon. From end to end, this one structure cut out the world. Spires reached up toward the perpetual storm overhead. A keep the size of a mountain stretched even higher, each level holding a slightly smaller rectangular section of stone until Gaeron lost count.

So many places to hide.

The distance felt reachable now. Which was good, because Gaeron could make out details of the Skinless now. They were no longer an ambiguous cloud or a blurry wall of white. Distance still obscured their numbers, but he didn't need specifics. Hundreds chased them—too many to fight. That was all that mattered. Their white frames, devoid of life but animated, shook. Chasing, their arms and legs moved in jerks and starts. Gangly as they were, he could break maybe fifty before he fell, but hundreds more would still swarm his best friend and the Chaos Bender he was here to protect. Being blood in the sand was one thing. Dying a senseless death was another.

"We have to run. Now!" He snagged Drulf's wrist and threw his arm over his shoulder. If the move helped or hurt, he couldn't tell, but time had run out.

They were halfway to the palace when the rattling of bones became sharper, the clanking of steel became clear, and the smack of onyx against onyx, unmistakable.

He craned his head. Individual skeletons, in full detail, greeted his analysis. Each was armed. Most held black onyx swords and cudgels. Some carried maces. Others were armed with spiked clubs. A few held rusted steel. All could kill.

Chali panted.

He drew his own deep breath, never feeling like he could catch it.

"I'm sorry, Gaeron," Drulf said.

"Shut up. The more you talk, the less oxygen you have to run."

Two hundred yards from the palace, the black sand hardened under his feet. Time had blown the sands over something below. A street. He didn't worry about the accuracy of his guess, but used it to their advantage as they raced along.

The sand remained firm and they put distance between themselves and their pursuers.

"Careful," he warned, "we can't take a chance of slipping."

An arrow bounced off the sand ahead, shifting it to reveal the marble below.

Within bowshot. Something Gaeron hadn't thought to consider. The Skinless army were using archers now. Why? Did their proximity to the palace unnerve the skeletons? Were the undead trying to stop them from reaching it? Why? Was this an instinctual reaction by the horde or were they capable of strategic thought?

All Gaeron knew was that they had to get inside the palace or die trying.

Gaeron unwrapped Drulf's arm, nudging Chali. She looked at him, confused. "Take him. Help him get to the palace."

Chali moved underneath the Buk Toh's arm, her eyes searching Gaeron's face. "What are you going to do?"

Gaeron pulled his battleax from its strap and faced the threat. "I'm going to slow them down. Go!"

"Gaeron—"

"Go!" he screamed, shifting the battleax and running forward to prevent the Chaos Bender from arguing further.

He wasn't sure how far she got before he cut down the first three Skinless. They were faster than the rest and were broken because of it. More came, and he slashed at them, breaking them as well.

One Skinless blurred into the next, and Gaeron lost count of how many empty frames he shattered. Each time his battleax smashed into bone, Gaeron's blade cracked and broke the enemy. Bloodlust rose inside him. Not born of skin and ligament, nor the iron taste of another man's blood. His was fueled by violence and destruction. Fed. Never satiated until nothing remained. Though this wasn't as satisfying as cutting flesh, he raged. The battleax, an extension of his spirit, endowed him with the rewards of his efforts. Severed arms and hands. Shattered ribs and spines. Smashed skulls.

An arrow cracked open the skull of the skeleton before him. Gaeron pulled back, surprised that the archers still fired even though their kind was upon him. That they'd risk their own to get to him only stoked his urge to kill even more.

Destruction embraced.

He swung his ax savagely but always under control, always thinking strikes ahead. The skeletons just attacked. They didn't think. They weren't strategic. They came at him with all their force. The mass of their army would soon join the early arrivers. Gaeron, filled with bloodlust or not, couldn't defeat hundreds.

Still fighting off the creatures of bone, he backed toward the palace. They pressed forward, arriving in larger and larger clumps, each cut down.

Back, back, back, they pushed him. None came close to scratching him. Too many bowed around him, their crescent taking shape. Within a few more strides, they'd fully encircle him if he didn't act now. He slashed and smashed five times his number with every swing. They fell at his feet as the shadow of the Black Palace loomed.

"Down, Gaeron!" Chali shouted behind him.

He dropped to the ground, trusting that she wouldn't allow the sea of Skinless to devour him. As soon as he hit the sand-covered marble, a blast flew through the first ranks, blowing undead backward in shredded pieces.

With one spell, Chali broke ten times the numbers he had with all of his fighting.

"Now, run!"

Gaeron scrambled to his feet and sprinted toward the palace. A black mouth yawned open. Somehow, Chali and Drulf had found a way inside. Not caring how, he ran as the clattering and clinking of armed Skinless regained lost ground.

He dove into the open maw and helped Drulf slam the heavy stone door shut.

A fixed silence swallowed him. Only their combined breaths filled the space. The enraged rattling outside was cut off.

"Now what?" Drulf huffed.

"Now we rest," Chali said.

Neither Bound Boy argued.

7

KARADEHTI

LITTLE IN HER desert life made Karadehti feel alive if it didn't have a cock attached to it. Right now, she was very alive.

She rolled to her right side, reaching out and grasping Rek's manhood, limp but still thick. He was going to father a quarter of Olma-Ka's next generation as more Freed women heard about his physical blessings. "Are you ready again?"

He pulled the long stick of ox jerky from his mouth, dark bits caught between his teeth. This man was lucky to be sharing her tent. "Give me a moment to gather my strength, Karadehti. You are insatiable."

The jerky slid towards his lips when she would rather her parts be wrapped in his lips. Maybe teeth too. Yes, teeth would be good.

She sighed and rolled to her left side, grabbing Nulot's cock. He was smaller, not as thick or satisfying, but still larger than most Freed men she had lain with. "What about you?"

Nulot blinked. "You've already drained me of my seed three times. Would you turn me to dust?"

Karadehti was ready to let him know that if he could have her with child by the time he was done, then she would gladly set that condition on him. She sat up. The air inside her tent was still. A rivulet of sweat rolled down her spine. "Hand me the goblet."

The Bound Boy attending her, Abrot Jelso, was wonderfully dutiful. Karadehti had known his parents, both killed earlier in the year while hunting. Though it was an accident, accidents didn't put food in the kid's mouth or maintain his tent. He was too young to manage adult tasks on his own. In the Olmarian way, the village pitched in to ensure his young life wasn't wasted. Though their communal effort would help him survive, he would never thrive unless he had work, so she had hired him as her attendant. The boy took to tasks quickly and without reservation, which was exactly what she needed. At eleven, he was hardly ignorant to the ways of women and men. Around Olma-Ka, he would have seen the activities at the Bed of Petals, which writhed with nude bodies any day it wasn't too miserably hot to fuck. He would have been at feasts where the Circle of Fire became an open orgy. When she explained that his duties would include attending to her when she had men in the tent, he was unflappable.

Karadehti had laughed and pinched his ears that flapped outward like bird wings, and gave him his first gold coin on the spot.

Abrot had held true to his word since that day—a wise investment and a saving grace for the boy. He would make a great Freed man one day, she was sure. In fact, she would help him how she could.

Abrot carried a tray of goblets for her and the two men. Nulot reached to grab his, taking the one in the middle. He handed it to Karadehti, staring at her breasts. Taking his next, he let Rek fend for his own. Abrot leaned across the cot so the second man could reach the tray.

Nulot slapped Abrot on the ass, a sharp sound. The boy jerked, shooting straight up. His eyes widened, and he held the tray as if he were a carved statue, his eyes fixed on the far tent wall.

"Are you going to join us?" Nulot asked.

Karadehti sipped her mead, staring at Abrot from over the top of her goblet. He was unsettled. "Leave him alone. Abrot, can you please bring me a handful of grapes? I'm famished."

Rek's hand was on her thigh when the boy turned away. "Are grapes the only thing you need to satiate your hunger?"

Karadehti gave him a sly smile. "I thought you were turning to dust?"

"He's just playing for you," Nulot said, dipping back his goblet and emptying it. "He wants to be the man known for putting a baby in Karadehti Tiaso."

The comment would have bothered many women to the point they would have shoved a dagger in Nulot's throat. It tweaked her nerves as well, but she was so practiced with the issue that she easily stifled her reaction. As much of an ass as Nulot was being, he was a terrific lover and not at all wrong. The first man to give her a child would become a living legend. Everyone in Olma-Ka would agree. Her struggles were legendary, talked about even in many meetings with the elders, and spoken about when the Freed women came together. For most people though, concerned with the daily struggle to survive and thrive in the Olka-Fa, the issue was the least of their concerns, and had faded to the periphery.

For everyone except me and Nydera.

Nydera cared too much about the issue because she felt Karadehti didn't care enough. But what was she supposed to do? At this point in her life, she should have already borne two or three children, ensuring her legacy and family heritage. As it was, she had no more status than a Freed woman killed in her first battle. In the eyes of fellow Olmarians, that's where she would rest forever unless she found herself with child one day.

Now, lying on her cot between the two naked men, their

seed still draining from her, Karadehti felt the flush of annoyance. When Abrot returned with the tray of grapes, she gave him a friendly smile. Softly, she said, "Abrot, take my goblet and refill it."

The boy extended the tray.

"Take theirs as well," she said, feeling the men's eyes on her.

"Are we to leave?" Rek asked.

"Yes."

Silently, the men crawled from the bed and dressed. Karadehti stole a few more glances at their naked bodies as she fed herself the juicy grapes. They were fine men, and either of them giving her offspring would ensure she had a strong child. But the gods were cruel, and her time with them would likely serve as nothing more than a way to pass another hot day. She wasn't disappointed when they slipped their red robes on and took their leave.

Karadehti gestured at the tent flap, annoyed by the smell of their sex filling the space. "Tie that open. The smell of men is pungent. I will lose my status if my sword sister thinks they have dominated me." She tried to make the comment sound light, but it came off flat.

Abrot did as she'd ordered, turning to ask," Am I to leave too?"

Karadehti got out of bed, standing naked before the boy. "I'm going to go to the bathing pool. Would you join me? The day is hot; this tent hotter still. You've worked hard and deserve to have fun. Maybe a girl or three will be bathing? Maybe Hana? Wouldn't that be a pleasant end to your day?"

The boy's face lit with excitement. "I would like that very much. Thank you."

"You're welcome, Abrot," Karadehti said, pulling her red robe over her head and straightening it before slipping on sandals. A warm trail of seed slid down her leg. She needed to get outside the tent before she dripped it all over the carpet. Ages ago, a merchant from Xandar had come through the village, and Karadehti was fat with coin from a recent raid on a Buk Toh caravan. She'd overpaid for the carpet but the last laugh was hers, because fifteen sun cycles later, it looked as vibrant as the day she'd bought it. "I really appreciate you. I just want you to know that."

Abrot's widened eyes shot glances toward the tent door. "Thank you, Karadehti. It is a great honor to serve you."

"And you are a great servant." She smiled, moving closer and draping her arms around the boy's neck. He was shaking. Adorable. Pinching his white robe's neckline, she straightened it. "But let's stop using that word, shall we? You're not a servant at all. You are my attendant and a damn good one at that." She stopped when she noticed his gaze shoot to the tent flap again. "What's wrong?"

His gaze skipped away. "Nothing, Karadehti."

"Something is bothering you."

"May I speak honestly?"

"Of course. You may always say your peace openly and honestly with me, Abrot. Know that."

"Thank you." He swallowed and lowered his head. "Those men... I don't like them."

Karadehti stifled her chuckle. "Oh? Why not?"

Abrot's eyes never left the tent floor. "They don't treat you with respect."

A sweet boy, but not a boy of the world. She would make an Olmarian man of him one day. Just not now. He wasn't ready for the lessons she taught. Instead, Karadehti released his collar and rested her forearms on his shoulders, her hands draped over his back. Thin shoulders. Those of a boy. When he didn't look up, she curled a finger under his chin and gently encouraged him. When his eyes met hers, she said, "Those men treat me the way I allow them to treat me. Never forget that, Abrot. A Freed woman is treated as she allows herself to be. Remember that, okay?"

He swallowed again and nodded.

"Good," she said, spinning him and giving him a nudge toward the door. "Now let's get to that bathing pool. I feel disgusting."

The waters were too warm and not at all refreshing. Still, Karadehti felt renewed. Re-energized. Abrot had moved off to seek his own conquests. The gods were kinder to him than they had ever been to Karadehti. Hana was at the bathing pool, splashing and kicking around with four other girls. Abrot and two of his friends joined the fun, laughing and playing, their young, naked bodies unscarred by desert life.

"Enjoy your youth. The desert never yields," she whispered before climbing out of the bathing pool and dressing.

The waters never touched her unsettled mind. The men hadn't either. She thought a few hours of animalistic sex would have freed her, at least for a short time. But it hadn't.

Many things occupied her mind, such was the burden of the Paramount's sword sister. Besides her own personal issues, Karadehti accepted carrying Nydera's the moment they swore to spend the rest of their lives as sisters.

Foremost was the scene at the trench project. Hanging over her like the unforgiving sun, she couldn't put the troubling thoughts from her mind. Karadehti loved Nydera more than anyone in Olma-Ka, even the ghosts of her parents. As an only child, she didn't have kin to call her own, and even if she did, Nydera would still hold a higher station. The Paramount was a sword sister in the truest sense of the title.

And the Paramount was naïve.

Nevilan was up to something. Had she not worried for the stain on Nydera's claim as Paramount, Karadehti would have snuck into the Two-Marked man's tent the night they caught him holding counsel with the Bound Boys at the trench. The Freed man hadn't been avoiding work. Scheming, was more like it. Like many senior Freed, he was moving subtly. Moving Bound Boys. Positioning them. But for what purpose? Without a doubt, he was devising something; something dark. Whatever his intentions, they didn't involve Nydera's best interests, or even the best interests of other Olmarians. Nevilan was about Nevilan alone, and no one else. He always had been, and he always would be. Even as a youth, she had watched his early years when the Andel family was a healthy, tight unit. Nevilan stood out then as a bad seed and only worsened after he and Gaeron lost their parents. While Gaeron's childhood showed signs of exceptionalism, Nevilan's was filled with mediocrity and angst. She was sure he had developed a dislike of women even before the first hair sprouted on his balls.

Nydera gave him too many chances, as she did with many of the troubled Olmarians. She was a thinker and didn't act for the sake of acting. Nydera avoided action until she could no longer. One day, that would cost her. Determined to set a different course for Olmarians, to make sure the old ways didn't become the new, Nydera was also binding herself with her inaction. Those who opposed the new fortifications, elders or not, needed to be taught a lesson. But the woman wouldn't raise steel to them. When they were alone at night, Nydera would talk about her insane idea to free all the Bound Boys, her dislike of binding them at the first sign of puberty was that strong. Only in those quiet, confident conversations did the Paramount admit that she feared too many would oppose such a measure and that another Freed woman might make the claim if for no other reason than to stop the Freeing of all boys. Nydera didn't fear someone making the claim, Karadehti knew that. But she also wouldn't put the stockade project at risk. Once it was finished?

Well, that was a long time off. Nydera would surely face another hundred troubles by then. Troubles, like the ones Nevilan Andel was likely plotting now.

As her sword sister, Karadehti would act where Nydera wouldn't.

She fingered the pommel of her dagger as she crossed the village, past rows of tents, each a higher status than the previous. Across the Circle of Fire, she stomped past those with more social privilege and into the lower ranks until she reached the tent belonging to Rercan Pyard, Nevilan's most trusted sidekick.

She yanked the tent flap open and peered inside. A single candle burned well below the coiled metal spring, down to the candle holder. Rercan was asleep on his cot, his head turned, profiling his large, hooked nose. Karadehti checked her surroundings and slipped inside, drawing her dagger. She straddled him, pinching his arms with her muscular legs, and the dagger at his throat before he woke.

This one will never be Freed, she thought as she leaned closer, smelling his sweat.

Rercan sniffed when he woke. "Karadehti? What... what are you doing?"

His throat bobbed underneath the dagger blade, scratching his skin, drawing small dots of blood.

"I'm here to get the truth," she said.

"What truth?"

His arms twitched. He was testing to see how much freedom he had.

Karadehti squeezed her legs that still quivered from her earlier fun and pressed the blade, sending a clear signal. If she wasn't happy with what he said, he would regret it. "What was Nevilan talking to you about at the trench when you and that group of boys should have been working?"

"Nevilan?" Rercan said the name as if it were a foreign word. "He... I don't remember, Karadehti. Why? What happened?"

"Nothing happened... yet," she said, hanging over him menacingly, using her free hand to brace herself against his shoulder and pressing down. "But I can't promise you something won't in the next few moments if you aren't honest."

Rercan swallowed again. "I... I honestly don't know what you're talking about."

She pressed. A thin line of red appeared. "This is not a game, boy. What was he talking about with you and the other Bound Boys?"

"I swear, Karadehti, he wasn't saying anything wrong. Just... just complaining."

Karadehti lightened the pressure on his throat, keeping the blade against his skin. "Complaining about what?"

"Just the work." A nervous smile flickered on Rercan's lips. "You know how he can be. He doesn't like physical labor. Just that. About how hot the day was. About us even having to do it. He thinks... he thinks the Paramount is being cowardly by building whatever the ditch is supposed to be. Doesn't matter to him if it's to help defend the village. That's all, Karadehti. I swear."

Karadehti searched his face. Rercan was such a weakling she had difficulty telling if he was being deceitful or just scared out of his wits. For all she knew, this could be both the full truth as the scrawny boy saw it and a partial truth because he was too stupid to scheme without plotting. Rercan wasn't the type to full-out lie; he wasn't smart enough.

"That's all he did? Just complain about the work? Then why did he rebel against Leonaime when all she was doing was her job of getting your lazy asses back to work?"

"I... I don't know why he did that. He's just Nevilan, Karadehti. Everyone knows he thinks highly of himself. Maybe she embarrassed him when she yelled? I don't know. I swear, he was just griping. I think the hot day got to him."

"Maybe we need to double the work details for the bunch of you. That will harden soft boys."

Rercan's eyes widened. "But... but... I did nothing. We were just listening. He is Two–Marked. We're Bound Boys. We can't exactly ignore him. He knows that. Please, talk to the Paramount. Don't double our details. We did nothing wrong."

Karadehti sat up straight, pulling the dagger away from Rercan's throat. "You better be speaking true words." She pointed the dagger tip at his nose, pressing the point against his skin, indenting it. "Because if you're lying to me, this will be the first thing I cut off. Slowly."

Rercan didn't move, didn't even nod. He lay perfectly still until she was off him and leaving his tent.

Frustration walked beside her back to her tent. Something wasn't sitting right. Rercan was a dumb boy, too dumb to see Nevilan's plans. He could have been completely honest with her and still absolutely incorrect about the older Andel boy. The Two–Marked Freed man was trouble. But what sort of trouble? For whom?

She was a row away from her tent when Karlli Thorst, a Freed man in his forties, crossed her path. He carried the leg of a pig. She stopped him. "Where are you headed?"

Karlli lifted the pig leg. "I have cook duty tonight." He wiggled the leg in the general direction of the Circle of Fire.

She grabbed him by the collar of his robe, dragging him toward her tent. "You'll cook soon enough. First, there's something I need you to attend to."

This time, Karadehti didn't hold back her moans of ecstasy, allowing the whole of Olma-Ka to hear her release.

8

NEVILAN

NEVILAN KNEW he should have been drinking more water than mead, but his mind was troubled, his body sore, and his every movement reminded him of the toll the days were taking on him.

Blackness gripped the world. Heat loosed itself from the desert floor, breaking free and drifting toward the heavens. Olma-Ka settled into another evening of rest and recuperation, recovering from the taxing day. Part of him couldn't help but wonder if Nydera pushed the men so hard so they wouldn't realize the unfair burden they shouldered. Why not? Olmarian men had been for generations.

The ditch project had now passed the northwest watchtower, thanks to the efforts of the Bound Boys and the few Freed men who joined them. Leonaime Nynar had caused him trouble three new suns ago by her antics, trying to assert her superiority. Superiority only given to her by the fact she was born with a cunt instead of a cock. Still, the confrontation had set him back. The Bound Boys were unnerved by her bold actions, forcing him to spend the following days slowly rebuilding their confidence in his vision.

It was so easy to reset the way fearful people thought, a

factor he would have to plan to address throughout this struggle. Leonaime wouldn't be the last woman to challenge his station. The incident at the ditch wouldn't be the last time she, or another Freed woman, reminded the Bound Boys and many Freed men of their inferior status. None of them seemed capable of counteracting the oppressive nature of the Olmarian culture. He would lead them from that. He would lead them into a new way of life, for Olma-Ka's men and boys. Few saw what they deserved, what had been unjustly taken from them when their mothers still had them swaddled in protective arms. A time would come when he would show them.

The wheels of that movement were already in motion.

"Are you ready?" Rercan asked, sitting in the sand, facing the Circle of Fire.

Atop the driftwood bench he chose not to share this evening, Nevilan answered, "Not yet. I'm waiting."

"For what?"

"We're not going alone."

If Rercan was curious what he meant, he didn't ask. The pair passed the time without idle chatter, for which Nevilan was grateful. There were so many moving parts to this next step they consumed him. Just when he was sure how to proceed, new factors sprang up, demanding consideration. As he cleared those, even more possibilities replaced them. So many.

Never admitting the possibilities were overwhelming, Nevilan knew they were bogging him down. Movement forward was stalling. Off-course was not a destination he had planned for, and it had happened so quickly. All because of the old bitch and sneaky Paramount.

Now was the time to focus on the path. Tonight, moments from now, he would take the next step and return to the path.

Footsteps approached.

"Sorry I'm late. I got caught cleaning the pit after dinner," Tocan said as he stepped out of the shadows.

Nevilan stood. Black soot covered Tocan. His face was so filthy, Nevilan couldn't tell where the soot ended and the tall man's shadow of facial hair began. Completely unpresentable. But they didn't have time to worry about the Bound Boy with the permanent sneer cleaning himself up. So much had to get done while it was safe, while they wouldn't draw attention.

"Let's go," Nevilan said and the Bound Boys jumped to follow. "And keep quiet."

Olmarians were engaged in typical post–dinner activities, settling in for the night to start the day as soon as first light appeared. But tonight was not for settling. Nevilan and his companions had grander tasks to accomplish than resting for another day of slave labor.

The two Bound Boys followed closely behind, neither speaking, just as he had ordered. They couldn't afford attention. Prying eyes and ears had ruined his move at the project. He'd deny them that tonight.

A different guard stood watch at the cage. This one was as wide as he was tall, not an impressive Olmarian specimen, which surprised Nevilan. Rercan had scouted earlier to see who was on guard duty, and told Nevilan of this man's story, but this wasn't what he'd expected. According to his hawk-nosed friend, the guard, Chiesasa, had been injured three sun cycles before in a training accident, and hadn't been able to walk correctly since. Only a One-Mark before the injury, he would likely remain one forever now. Based on what Nevilan saw before him, the injury hadn't done any favors for the man's status among Olmarians or his health. Shocked that Nydera would expose the prisoner to any guard who didn't immediately strike fear in someone's eyes, he no longer had to worry about a confrontation tonight.

"What do you want?" the wide man asked as the three approached.

In the flickering firelight, Nevilan noted the single triangular mark on the man's forehead. He pulled back his long curls, exposing his Marks to stop any further questions from this lower man. "I'm here to talk to the prisoner."

"About what?" the guard asked.

Nevilan leaned closer to the fire, tapping his two triangular scars. "It is not your place to question me."

The comment seemed to surprise Chieasa, who shifted back. When he spoke, he did so with less confidence. "My duty is to guard the prisoner."

"And guard him, you are," Nevilan said, giving the guard's body a critical analysis, curling his upper lip. With two good legs, this man would be dangerous. Limited as he was, he would have to be smart, unless he wanted to feel Nevilan's wrath. "He isn't going anywhere. Good for you, I'd say. You wouldn't be able to chase him back to the Circle of Fire. Worry less about me and more about where you've failed your people by..." Nevilan sneered, waving an arm at the man's body, "doing that to yourself. Now, I will speak with him."

He rounded the cage, eyeing Taowen while the merchant wore a quizzical expression. The torches flickered, casting orange light bright enough for Nevilan to catch the merchant sliding his gaze toward the guard. The smell of burning grease irritated his nose. Reminding himself to stay composed, Nevilan could not deny his excitement. A pathetic guard on-duty was the gods' way of blessing him.

Or sending me a clear signal.

Shielding the guard's view by keeping his back to him, Nevilan reached to his belt and untied his mead skin. Stretching his arm through the cage, he offered it to Taowen, who took it.

The merchant uncorked the skin, smelled its contents, and closed his eyes. "I swear, the longer I am imprisoned here, the better your shit mead smells." He raised the skin in a salute and drank.

Nevilan watched.

After he drank, Taowen stood and held the skin without replacing the cork. "I'll be finishing this before we're done with our conversation. I appreciate it."

Nevilan dipped his head. "As soon as I can get access to the Freed stores without drawing attention, I can bring you better mead. Though, I hope that will be unnecessary."

Taowen cocked his head.

"I've kept an open ear to see what I could learn about your situation, and I'm afraid to report I have found little," Nevilan said. "I'm afraid the Paramount is either being very quiet about her plans for you, or she doesn't have any. Neither of which bodes well. I don't imagine you're enjoying suffering through our long days in this." He raised his hands toward the cage.

Taowen nodded repeatedly, turning away slowly. "She has her plans, but it seems I'm frustrating her at every turn."

"Oh? She has finally revealed something to you?"

Taowen barked a laugh. "She wants a day when I become an Olmarian merchant, if you will." He held his hands out to his side in an apologetic gesture. "I realize I am Buk Toh. Is that not how you refer to us in your tongue?"

"It is."

"And your Paramount seems to think I can somehow help the village in this capacity, promising me more freedom. More, not complete, if I cooperate. Regardless, I imagine I will forever remain her prisoner," Taowen said.

"How sure of this are you?" Nevilan asked, concerned to learn Nydera was already communicating her plans with Taowen. Everything he had been laying out was under threat. Depending on what Nydera was offering, it wasn't unrealistic to think Taowen could betray the conversations they'd had. Yet Nydera hadn't come for him, nor had her nuisance of a sword sister. None of her guards. None of the lap dogs barked with their bladed threats. No, if the merchant had betrayed them, he would have already been dead.

Taowen took another swig. He pulled the skin away, laughing as mead dribbled through the deep crevices of age lines around his mouth and down his chin. "That bitch thinks to use me as a conduit to Merchant's Row. She expects me to serve as the name and face of goods traded from here to there. At a great profit, I might add. She's interested in coin only, and will keep me as a slave so that she can make as much as possible before the gods call me home. I'll see my end before I do that for her. She talks about a debt owed, but sees no problem in creating debts herself. I'll not help."

Rercan stepped to the cage. "But if you don't help, she could have you killed."

Taowen's crystal eyes burned. "Are you an imbecile, boy? If she kills me, your people's sacrifice was for nothing. No. She won't. She'll perpetuate this torture. But what she doesn't know is that the longer she keeps me caged like an animal, the less willing I am to help. I will do small things to curry favor and bide my time, but that is all." He squared on Nevilan. "My hope is that I don't have to wait long."

"You won't ," Nevilan said.

"Interesting." The comment sounded like a purr.

Nevilan noted the merchant's cautious tone. "We can help each other. But I need to know how I can help you." He held his arms out, slapping both Bound Boys on the back. "We are but three, but we are growing. I need to be careful, you understand."

Taowen said, "I'm listening."

"There are others, but we must be cautious," Nevilan continued.

"You're confident they can be useful?"

"Yes."

The merchant turned to check on the guard, lowering his voice. "How many?"

"No more than a handful." The merchant would expect honest answers. Nevilan would give them as long as they were useful.

Something flickered in Taowen's expression. A flinch, as if Nevilan's admission pained him.

"It has to start somewhere. This is our start. A new way forward for Olmarians." Nevilan's confidence grew with each word. "Imagine, being part of our new history from the very beginning? Imagine the relationships we might build together. Having a say in where we start and where we go. Having future generations see you as a savior. No amount of coin could be traded for such privileges and prestige... but there would be enough to make it more than worth someone's time."

Taowen paced the flattened sand. He waved the mead skin in the air. "What you say has promise. There is much potential in your words. Words that, may I say, will earn you strong friends and powerful enemies."

"I understand that."

"Are you ready for that?"

"I'm ready for my people to be free," he responded with full conviction.

"Yes." Tocan growled at his side.

"There may be a way," Taowen said, moving to the side of the cage, separated from Nevilan only by the wood bars.

Nevilan kept his face straight. The merchant had been neglected during his imprisonment, smelling of musk, sweat, and piss. "Name it."

"When they abducted me from my headquarters, I carried a small satchel."

"What does it contain?" Nevilan asked.

"Coin," Taowen said with a cocky sneer. "Not that I expect it to still hold them. But, coin can be replaced. The satchel contained other items that are of no apparent worth, but which I need. Business information, shall we say?"

"Is that all?"

"No. There is something else that will help. Something that would free me so that I can repay your kindness."

"What?"

Taowen straightened. "Bring me the satchel. If all is in order, I will show you the key that will help you liberate your people."

The two men stared at each other for a long moment. Tocan rubbed his dry hands and Rercan shuffled from foot to foot. The small fire that kept the guard warm crackled until Nevilan pushed all the noise so far away they flickered out. The void became his connection with the merchant, the man who could hand Nevilan the power he needed to change his fate.

To become Paramount.

"I will do it," Nevilan said, as nervous excitement flared through him.

Taowen lifted the mead skin in a last toast. "When you have, you know where to find me."

The merchant turned away, moving closer to the guard's fire. He blew into his hand.

Nevilan backed away from the cage.

"Nevilan," Rercan's whisper contained an even level of trepidation and hostility. "What he speaks of, we cannot do. This is treason."

But Nevilan looked past his shorter friend with the thick blanket of matted black hair to Tocan. He gave the tall man a stiff nod. The signal. Tocan split off in the opposite direction as Nevilan rounded the cage to address the fat guard. "Watch over the prisoner and report any visitors to me."

The guard's chubby face scrunched. "Why would I do that?"

"I will make it worth your effort."

At that, the guard bobbed on the balls of his feet. "Will you, now? Lucky me."

"Yes. Name your price."

Rercan tugged at Nevilan's robe. The Two-Marked man swatted away the invasive hand. "We cannot do this. We—"

"Five golds a day," the guard said. "I work tonight and again in two new suns. Tomorrow, I'm in the damned ditch. Heard the pathetic Bound Boys have been slacking off. I can talk to the other guards and switch a sh—"

The wide guard never saw Tocan, never saw the soot-covered Bound Boy draw his dagger. Never saw the hungry look in Taowen's eyes, watching from behind the bars. The only man to witness tonight's meeting who Nevilan didn't trust, at least in part, never saw the threat until the blade drew a red line of death deep into his neck, severing ligaments and his esophagus.

A river of red ran down the guard's throat, covering the front of his robe before his hands moved from his belt. His wide eyes locked on Nevilan as he collapsed to his knees before falling face-first to the sand.

"The gods will curse you," Rercan spit at Tocan.

"Silence!" Nevilan spun on his smaller friend, grabbing him by the robes and pressing him against the cage bars. "Unless you want to be silenced forever as well, you won't speak of this. Understand?"

Rercan nodded, tears forming in the corners of his eyes. "I... I d—do. Bu—but why, Nevilan? Why?"

Tocan moved closer, the dagger still in his hands.

Nevilan released Rercan. "Because he would have betrayed us. Betrayed our purpose. The situation requires fidelity."

"This is what happens to anyone who betrays us," Tocan said.

Rercan's hurt eyes never left Nevilan even as Tocan threatened him.

"Bu—but I... I would never betray you," Rercan whimpered.

Nevilan put a single hand on Rercan's robe, softly straightening it. "See that you don't. It would tear me apart inside if you were to betray me, and I would hate to lose you."

Looking at the dead guard, Taowen sipped from the mead skin before pulling his lips back in a satisfied grin. "This is a promising start."

"This is just the beginning of a future that holds more than promise," Nevilan said.

9

GAERON

THE NIGHT WAS DAY. Day was night. The one, the same as the other. Time, endlessly blending. Had they missed a new sun? Two? There was no way to tell. No way to know. Not for sure.

At first, the small chamber inside the Black Palace cut out the noise of the skeleton army. As they sat, as they stretched, as they paced the small room, the noise outside the chamber walls grew.

Rattling of thousands of bones. Rattling of onyx weapons against the black stone walls. Thumping. Thumping. Thumping. The sound of a hundred, two hundred or more, skeleton fists smashing against stone three times as thick as an adult, in order to get to the living.

Chali slammed her hand against the stone. The smack was sharp this close, but the thick walls absorbed it instantly. "Will you just sleep, you brainless beasts!"

Drulf laughed, half asleep. "They can't hear you."

"How do you know?"

Drulf shrugged, placing a hand over his growling stomach and grimacing. "They don't have ears."

Silence. Then Chali snorted so loudly her amusement filled the small chamber.

"I deserve that," she said, and then pointed at Drulf's stomach. "You should eat."

Drulf lifted his pack, wiggling it. The small flame Chali had started from the dry vines littering the chamber lit one flat side of the pack. "I have to be careful."

"Where are your supplies?" Gaeron asked.

Drulf patted his stomach. "The answer to that can be found within. Most of them, anyway."

"You were supposed to be careful before you needed to be," Chali chastised, leaning over to grab her sack, placing it in her lap. She untied it, reached in and pulled out a square of tack, breaking it in half. "Here."

Drulf waved it away. "No. No. I can't."

"You must."

Drulf looked around the small chamber to the far side, still within the flames reach. "We don't know how long we'll be here. I don't want to take a chance." He shimmied down the wall, placing his sack under his head and adjusted his shoulders as if he was digging them into the stone floor. "Sleep helps. When you're asleep, you don't realize how hungry you are."

"He has a point," Gaeron said, finding Chali's concerned eyes. "Plus, we'll need his strength as much as his brains to find a way out of this chamber and into the palace itself."

"What guarantee do you have that it'll be free of the Skinless?" Chali asked. "Only those we broke stopped attacking, and by the sounds on the other side of this stone." She tapped the wall with her thumb. "My guess would be that the sun has slept, and the broken have regenerated. They're louder, in case you didn't notice. When the sun wakes, if it hasn't already, we don't know for sure they'll stop. They're eternal as long as that magic animates them. We're not. One step outside and they'll tear us to meaty pieces."

Gaeron grimaced. "Nice thought."

The chamber had revealed no secrets. Chali was burning

everything flammable, which wasn't much, thickening the air as it did. At this rate, it wouldn't be long before they wouldn't be able to see their hands in front of their faces. The thick door, made of the same stone as the floor and walls, was heavy and barred. The latter looked as if it had been installed ages ago, but the brackets held up, showing no signs of giving up the constant assault. The Skinless weren't coming in unless they knew another way, and Gaeron didn't fear the brainless creatures figuring that out. Still, they couldn't stay here for long. The dried vine was burning slowly, but it was still burning and there wasn't much left. Next, they'd have to start burning anything they could, including their clothes and contents of their sacks. Without light, running out of food and water, the undead wouldn't have to worry about tearing into the humans. Time would do that at its own torturous pace.

"We can't stay in here," Gaeron whispered once Drulf was asleep. In the darkness, he was unsure if Chali was still awake. The flame from the burning vine had faded to cool flickers well after Drulf started snoring. If she was asleep, her constant movements hinted it was a restless one.

Sleep did not visit Gaeron. He couldn't get comfortable in the small chamber. He laid, he curled, he stood. Gaeron tried everything to loosen the knotting muscles and close his eyes for a few precious hours. Pacing the room was out of the question, with Drulf stretched out. At six and a half feet tall, he could almost span the room in this prone position.

The ancient brick kept the chamber cool, and as the hours stretched on, the coolness shifted to a persistent chill. Drulf's snoring sounded like the rare thunder that teased the edge of the desert.

And then there was the blasted Skinless, ceaselessly pounding against the stone from the outside. The simple creatures acted as if they thought to chip through the barrier. At the least, they were a determined terror. They'd drive him mad before they breached the palace, but that meant they'd still win in the end.

Only after Gaeron thought Chali had left him with his thoughts, she answered. Her voice was scratchy with exhaustion. "I know. Tomorrow... or... after sleeping. Sleep first."

Gaeron didn't answer, allowing her to rest without sharing his troubled thoughts. Sharing them wouldn't get them out of this predicament.

Chali drifted away while Drulf sounded as if he were combating an army of scorpions, the way he grunted and harrumphed and mumbled things that sounded like insults. Gaeron hoped that with the taxing race across the Dark Sands and the day's heat, the large man would have slipped into the deepest of sleeps. Instead, he tossed well past the time Chali fell into her sleep. Each time he heard her shiver, his adrenaline spiked. His fits finally stopped a while later, and the chamber fell into an eerie stillness. Except for the clattering outside, interrupted once by loud thumping that had Gaeron worried parts of the palace were tumbling down somewhere deep in its reaches. The world inside the chamber was at a stop.

The light of the fired vine began to die. If it did, he'd sleep in the dark. With Drulf already out, they didn't have to worry about him panicking at the lack of sight. With Chali also sleeping, lighting a torch was a waste. They each still carried a single torch, soaked in pig fat, and precious. The Paramount did what she could to prepare them for searching the confines of the Black Palace, but her knowledge was limited. They would be here as long as their rations remained. If they found sustenance and fresh water, they'd stay longer. Until they could be sure they'd have another light source, he wasn't going to light a torch to keep himself comfortable. When Chali's vine fire died, the chamber would go dark, and he'd deal with the consequences when the pair woke.

Not much later, as Chali's snores rivaled Drulf's, the fire

sizzled down to a single flame before finally going out. The darkness that followed was thick and oppressive, setting Gaeron on edge. He thought it wouldn't bother him, but it did. The night, if it was truly the time for the sun to sleep, stretched on. The feeling of the darkness pressing down on him became worse. He couldn't sit and listen to the army of Skinless on the other side of the wall any longer. He had to do something. The only distraction was to relaunch the search for an escape from it.

On his hands and knees, he passed the time by searching each brick for a clue, a trigger, something. The designers wouldn't have built this room without a way out, unless its only purpose was a prison. But that didn't make sense. They had accessed the room from the outside, racing across what had been a broad pathway of marble before finding this room. They had barred themselves from the inside, not outside. No, this was no prison.

Instead, Gaeron was confident this chamber was a secret entrance to the Black Palace. Somewhere, there was another way into the palace from this room. He simply had to find the way.

In the darkness, he couldn't tell if he was searching areas he'd already gone over. Maybe redoubling efforts would pay off, even if he was. Feeling cracks and crevices in the bricks for a latch, a loose stone, or a button that might trigger another door, Gaeron wouldn't be deterred. Even if he had searched the same area a fistful of times. He probably had, since the only point of reference he had were his two sleeping friends, and even they moved in their rest. Knowing his luck, the Buk Toh had rolled on the only device in the damned chamber that might provide an escape.

Then a thought dawned on him. Why couldn't that be true? After scouring the chamber and not finding anything resembling a release lever, he figured it might be hiding under Chali or Drulf. He didn't want to wake them, but he also didn't want to stay in here any longer than necessary. Chali was right. Opening the door to the outside would lead them straight into the hands of the Skinless and their superior numbers. After her rest, Chali could cast several powerful spells, but could she cast enough to keep the entire army occupied while Gaeron and Drulf broke them? He doubted that. Going back the way they had come in wasn't an option. He was missing something here.

Drulf's large form shifted, so Gaeron scurried to his friend. Placing his hands on the Buk Toh's back, Gaeron slowly pushed against the big man, encouraging him to roll over. Drulf did. Gaeron searched the stone, finding nothing.

Still encouraged he was onto something, Gaeron reached to find Chali in the darkness. When he did, he put a hand on her shoulder and one on the curve of her hip, and slowly turned her toward Drulf, trying to ignore the way her form dipped at her slender waist. He yanked his hand back as if her skin had burned, and placed it on her thigh. That wasn't much better. Oh, how she'd tease him if she knew. Drulf would too.

With Chali out of the way, he fingered the bricks where she had lain.

This part was as smooth and worn as every other spot. Gaeron was almost ready to climb the impassable walls to search the ceiling when he noticed a notch in a brick. In the darkness, his thick finger ran over the cut in the stone. An oddity. He pushed his finger deeper. The notch was smooth, set down from the rest of the block. More encouragingly, as he fingered it, the notch jiggled slightly.

Asking the gods for a favor, Gaeron pushed the notch. It sank.

From somewhere deeper in the chamber came a low rumbling sounded, growing louder. Drulf snorted. Chali gave a shivering breath and shifted in the darkness, mumbling something. The vine flickered with the orange light of a new flame, casting a weak light across a spot on the floor. He felt the first wisp of air.

That's why the flame intensified, he realized. Whatever he'd done had created enough of a draft to feed the fire, even slightly.

The wall a few feet away slowly shuddered, sending a cascade of dust falling from the ceiling to the floor as the door slid sideways at a crawl. Gaeron jumped to his feet, looking for his battleax, which lay on the opposite side of Drulf.

"Wha—what did you do?" Chali said in a sleepy but excited voice. She was getting to her feet as Drulf woke.

The big man rubbed his eyes with the palms of his hands. "What's happening?"

"We're getting out of here," Gaeron answered. "Get your things."

The pair were readied nearly as soon as he was, collecting their sacks, slinging them over their shoulders, and arming themselves. Chali gripped her truncheon. Drulf had his shortsword.

The full party awake, the Black Palace ready to be explored, Gaeron pulled out his torch, firebox and striker. "You started the last one. Let me see if I can get this going before we're in the dark again."

When he sparked the tinder and transferred it to the fat-soaked rags wrapped around the torch, light blossomed. Sharp stinging made Gaeron clamp his eyes shut and shield his face until they adjusted. When he pulled his arm away, he saw the Chaos Bender and Drulf both covering their faces. "Ready?"

Chali and Drulf's determined looks told him they were. The party moved out of the chamber and into a tight passageway with him leading the way.

"This won't be fun," Drulf said grimly as they stepped through the passageway filled with dust as old as Oltari.

Gaeron squirmed, thankful to be in front. The narrowness

of the passage pressed in, the ceiling dropping low. Half a foot taller than Gaeron, Drulf walked with a squat, forced down by the ceiling. Gaeron hurried as rapidly as was safe. They needed to get out of the passageway. Whatever was ahead had to be more attractive than spending a moment longer in these tight confines, though he didn't hear Chali complain.

"Do you see any more torches?" Chali asked. Still a whisper, her voice echoed.

Gaeron lifted the torch. The shadows ahead wavered. "That's the highest I can go.

"See anything?"

Gaeron peered into the darkness, seeing only the narrow passage stretching on. "Nothing. Let's keep going."

"Did you have another option?" Chali joked.

Gaeron scanned the walls far ahead for a sconce or torch. The black square ahead yawned, constantly shifting farther away as they pressed forward.

Their footsteps echoed, now so far from the chamber that they drowned out the scourge of Skinless who still hadn't given up. The drafty silence of the palace filled his ears, even as the pongy air filled his nostrils.

"I see one!" Gaeron spotted a torch hanging in a sconce on the wall.

"Just one?" Chali asked.

"Too dark. Light this one. Maybe we'll be able to make out more."

"I, for one, would really appreciate a long line of torches," Drulf said.

Gaeron could not disagree as he dipped his torch. This new one caught, almost too instantly. The circle of flickering light expanded. "Looks like this is our only one."

"Better than nothing," Chali said.

"With two of them, we should be able to find others and finally start this cursed search," Gaeron said.

"Let me take it and let's get going," Drulf said. "I want to get out of this passageway."

"Me too." Chali's voice was muffled as she turned back toward the chamber. "I don't like it, but I don't want to spend eternity in there. The only way is ahead. Let's get going."

Drulf pulled the torch from the sconce that hung level with his round shoulders. As soon as it was free, something clicked behind them. From the same direction of the chamber they'd abandoned. It sounded metallic, like giant slabs of metal being knocked together. The sound rippled outward, down the passageway, approaching. Fast.

"Run!" Chali ordered unnecessarily.

Gaeron was already nearing a sprint. Chali's feet were light, but Drulf already huffed.

"Keep moving!" Chali said in a panic.

Metal slammed against metal.

"It's close!" Chali warned.

Her voice was drifting farther back as Gaeron raced forward. They were separating, he realized. "Come on, we're almost at the end," he shouted.

"Good!" the Buk Toh said.

Their feet thundered ahead as the metallic smacking pursued from behind.

"How much longer?" the big man asked.

The metal-on-metal crashing closed, as if it came from right behind the party. It filled the passageway. In truth, Gaeron had no idea how much longer they had. Moments, at best. Another breath, at worst. He could do nothing for the two trailing him except continue sprinting into oblivion and lying about the distance to their destination.

"We're almost there."

"Where?" Chali shouted over the din.

Gaeron prayed to the gods the answer to that question would be uncovered soon. He also prayed he would live to apologize.

Just as he felt the air compress with each slam of metal–on–metal, Gaeron stepped through the passageway and into a large chamber.

"Here!" He turned and waved them forward.

Chali came through, followed by Drulf, tight on her heels. The trio pressed against the side wall and waited.

The approaching metal trap slammed to a stop at the end of the passageway, its ringing echoing far into this new room. Gaeron waited before peeling his back off the wall and stepping around the others to look back from where they had fled. Metal spikes, four-feet long, jutted from both walls. Had they not reached this large chamber, they would have been skewered. The spikes were thick and long enough to take down a sadeon.

Gaeron hid his shaking breath. In silence, the group stared at the spike trap.

"At least it would have been quick." Drulf winked.

"Quicker than you, that's for sure," Gaeron said.

"If you hadn't been so slow, I would have already been sitting down for my dinner meal in this... chamber," Drulf returned with a goofy smile.

Chali slapped the big man on the arm. "Let's check this place out and see what secrets... and threats, it holds."

They moved together, starting on the near wall and using it to guide them around. They kept their weapons at the ready, taking slow, deliberate footsteps forward. With no threat from behind, there was no reason to hurry and stumble into something else they might not be able to stumble out of again. Best to be careful and as quiet as possible.

Each wall of this large chamber, ten times as tall as the first chamber, held another arched doorway. They decided to explore the room before worrying about which hallway to journey down.

"We need to find the Crown of Spikes, not get lost in the Black Palace," Chali said.

The three covered every step of the larger chamber. Empty, not only of the crown, but of anything. This wretched place didn't even hold a single stool.

"Such a waste," Drulf said. "You could house half of Olma-Ka in this room alone, and yet these people used it for nothing?"

"Not for nothing," Gaeron said, pointing at the floor where a design of inlaid gold spread out from his feet, beyond the flickering torch flame. Long, straight lines stretched off into the darkness in all directions. There might have been a central point, but he didn't see one within the torchlight. Wandering farther, some of the things slowly curved outward while those in the middle blended into an oblong swirling oval. Did this represent the storm over the Dark Sands or something else. Whatever it was meant to convey, it did so with inlaid gold.

He was about to ponder how difficult it would be to wedge the gold free when the Buk Toh interrupted him. "What is that?"

Gaeron shrugged as he wandered around the design, partially awe-struck by what he was seeing. "I can't tell. It's far too big to see in this light, but it's impressive, whatever it is."

Chali stayed close, but she took careful steps that allowed her to see more of the art under their feet. Gaeron hid his smile when he noted how she stayed within the range of the torchlight as she examined the floor. "This could be a symbol of their gods. Maybe they used the chamber for religious purposes. Might explain why they'd need so much space. Best way to force all your subjugates to attend? Without better light, I can't tell what this is or what it's supposed to represent."

"It's not the Crown of Spikes," Gaeron said, pointing out the obvious. "So I say we keep moving."

Chali's face scrunched as she examined the design. "Agreed," she finally said.

"Which hall do we take?" Drulf asked.

Gaeron turned to take in the room's width, unable to see most of the arched doorways from the middle of the room. "Impossible to tell. I say we pick the one on the far right and work our way in a full circle from there, lighting everything in our path that can burn. I want to be able to see more than my own damn hands."

Chali gave a frustrated laugh. "I agree."

"How much luck do you think we'll have finding a wayward deer or even a desert fox trapped in one of these rooms? I could go for some meat. Anyone else tired of hard-tack?" Drulf said as they made their way down the first hall, finding sconces at equal intervals. Drulf used the torch to light the rest as they stretched into new reaches of the palace.

"The gods haven't shown us much luck yet, my friend. Save what you can of your tack and dried fruits just in case they continue to ignore us," Gaeron said as he searched.

Drulf patted his stomach. "Easier to crumble a mountain, stone by stone. You'll understand when you grow up, little friend, but it takes a lot of sustenance to make a man's body move."

The trio chuckled at Drulf's joke, moving deeper into the Black Palace.

10

KARADEHTI

Fucking was difficult when you had other things on your mind. Dark things. Things you couldn't put voice to without sounding as if the gods had twisted your mind. Karadehti already had enough struggles without adding to them.

Too late for that.

Favr Elto was a fit, reliable man who knew how to satiate her appetite, even temporarily. No man could permanently fulfill her, but there were a handful who could help her pass the long hours of the hottest part of midday with their corporal magic. What Favr could do with his hands and tongue was truly magical. Usually.

His typical level of skill was why she invited him today. But when he failed to fulfill her, she told him to recruit help, which he did with more than a bit of humiliation.

It wasn't his fault, Favr was an amazing lover. But frustration fed her hunger, something he couldn't understand or appreciate. She was pleasantly surprised when he returned with three Freed men.

Karadehti had seen them around the village, but two were only casual acquaintances. The third, Nrus Chalten, was one of Nydera's trusted sword trainers. Each time Karadehti saw him teaching the Paramount, she'd steal him for a few moments of innocent and not-so-innocent flirting. The way his seductive eyes remained pinched to narrow slits was intoxicating.

It was fun. Nrus was a humble man with a splendid physique and quiet intelligence. That made him different from most of the men in the village. At least the Freed ones. Karadehti disliked few people, and none of the protectors of her sword sister, but that didn't mean she enjoyed conversing with everyone. Nrus was very enjoyable, in more ways than one. Few were actually as stimulating mentally as they were physically. The times she spent speaking with him were always as thought-provoking as they were passionate. Nydera was lucky to have him.

And now Karadehti would in a different, more basic way.

The four men pleasured her for hours. Each had his own style, his own way of touching, his own way of devouring her essence. All four were good. All four would father strong children one day. Even when they took breaks to drink and re-energize, Karadehti remained on the cot with at least one. She wanted them to wear her out, to make her feel exhaustion like she had never felt. To tire her until she no longer had the desire to move. But as each of the four hardened and softened, repeating the cycle multiple times, a dark thought occurred to her. The circle of despair that routinely held her in its embrace, refused to let go. The reminder only grew more unyielding as sun cycles passed.

None would please her fully if they had from today until the end of the sun, because none of them could. She didn't blame them. All the Freed men in Olma-Ka wouldn't have satisfied her this day. The blame lay in her occupied mind. The mind reminding her each time she spread her legs for another man, the he, too, would fail in giving her a child.

She climbed out of the cot after Favr spent his seed for the fifth time. She crossed the tent naked, going to the table and pulling a handful of grapes free from their stem. She popped one into her mouth and bit. Its juices exploded inside her mouth, just as the men had a few times already today. Their eyes were on her, but she had grown tired of looking at them, of their presence. All of them except Nrus.

"Leave me," she said in a tired voice. "Not you, Nrus."

"Karadehti? Is everything all right?" he asked, his gorgeous, narrow eyes widening. "Have I not satisfied you?"

She watched as the other three dressed. They were fine men, men who would give a lucky woman or two strong offspring they could be proud of. For her, unless one of them was the most potent the gods had ever birthed into the world, they were nothing more than friendly toys. She regretted watching them prepare to leave, wishing they could be more a part of her life. But no man could be until she bore a child. The cruelty of the gods ensured she never would.

"Not at all," she answered after the men had clothed themselves. "I just want to talk for a moment."

In turn, each of the three approached Karadehti, kissing her lightly on the cheek. She thanked them, letting Favr linger longer than the other two. With him, she took a moment longer, rubbing him erect again before fully kissing him, slipping her tongue into his mouth, and sending him on his way.

He had a sheen to his face that hinted at his excitement. But being the good man he was, he dipped his head and slipped out of the tent, leaving her alone with Nrus.

He sat at the table, still naked, his dark skin glistening. He filled a goblet and smirked.

"What is that look for?" she asked.

Nrus tipped his head toward the tent flap. "You are a cruel mistress, Karadehti."

"Why is that?" she asked, knowing the answer.

"That poor man won't be able to think straight until he has rested."

"Good. Thinking men are dangerous men," Karadehti said, more truthfully than Nrus could know.

"All men can be dangerous," he said matter–of–factly. "Favr is a simple man with simple needs. There is little about him that is dangerous. Well, except the way he plays stones."

Karadehti wasn't familiar with the game. A Freed man's game she didn't have time for. Few Freed women took the time to learn it since it seemed like nothing more than a braggart's opportunity. But it helped the men pass time when they weren't working the fields, cooking the dinners, or digging Nydera's endless trench. The game kept them happy. As long as they still tended to their duties and were available for her, she didn't care how often they played. Even if the wives in the village complained.

"He has a temper?" she asked, half–interested. Favr was one of the most moderately tempered man she knew. It would surprise her to learn that he had angered over something as simple as a game.

Nrus laughed into his goblet. "Only when he loses. Beyond that, he can be fun to play with."

"I know," Karadehti said seductively.

"Cruel, cruel mistress," Nrus laughed. "What did you want to speak with me about? I hope I haven't upset you?"

Karadehti sat at the end of the table but moved her chair away from it. She sat, spreading her legs until the backs of her knees brushed the corners of the seat. Nrus's eyes never drifted down. Something inside her coiled. "Not at all. As always, my time with you is pleasurable. But I need help, and I trust few people. Even among the Freed. You, I feel I can share this secret with, and not worry about betrayal."

Nrus pulled back, his broad nose flaring. When he shrugged, the lean muscle of his chest constricted, deepening the valley between his pectorals. "Betray you? I would never do such a thing, Karadehti. No matter the secret."

How she longed to run a finger through that valley again.

Instead, she held up the finger. "Don't promise things you do not yet understand," she warned. "Hear me out first, and then we can see what you are made of."

"Of course. I'm sorry."

"Don't be." She put her hand on his firm tricep and let it slide down to his wrist. "I have to ask you something and I need complete honesty."

"Of course. Name it. If I can answer, I will do so in only true words."

She studied his face. Nrus would appreciate brevity. If she wanted him to be forthright with her, she needed to be so with him. "What are your thoughts about Nevilan Andel?"

"Nevilan?" Nrus said as if the name was one of the last he expected to hear. "Honestly, I have very little I think of him. He never crosses my mind. Why do you ask?"

Karadehti sat back, fingering the dwindling bunch of grapes in her palm. "I fear he is up to something."

"Something? Like what?"

She scrunched her forehead. "That's what I'm trying to figure out. Unfortunately, I'm not close enough to him to peel back the tent flap of his mind. I need someone who is."

"I'm afraid I can't help you there," Nrus apologized. "I've been Freed much longer than he, and I have a few cycles on him. We have rarely spoken. When we have in the past, it usually had to do with a work detail. Nothing personal. Not that I can recall. Of course, Nevilan is unremarkable. Easy to forget."

Now they were getting to the matter she needed to explore with him. "What about the other trainers or warriors? Would any of them be reliable? Does he have any friends among that kind?"

Nrus sat quietly, his sexy, narrowed eyes staring off as he ran his dark thumb down the side of the goblet. After a moment, he said, "Not that I can think of. The trainers, the warriors... aren't the type who would find a friend in someone like Nevilan."

She leaned forward, grabbing his arm again. "Speak freely with me, Nrus. You won't offend me. Your words are safe here."

Nrus flicked the side of the goblet with his thumbnail. His eyebrows angled down, almost merging above the bridge of his wide nose. "Fine, Karadehti. We don't like him. We don't trust him. We don't respect him. Nevilan will never have friends among us."

She nodded, relieved that at least the warriors wouldn't become a vulnerability Nevilan could use against Nydera.

"You're worried?"

Karadehti looked up from the grapes to his dark face. It was he who looked worried. She didn't know how long she'd been silent.

"Your words are safe here," he repeated her sentiment with a charming smile.

"My intuition tells me he is up to something, but I cannot figure out what. I needed to make sure he didn't have friends in the Freed warrior ranks who might cause problems. Your words have settled me, but I was hoping for something more."

"Like what?"

"An opening. I need a break. Most Olmarians either don't know him or don't like him. Those who do aren't speaking."

"I know one who might," Nrus said. He flinched at Karadehti's sudden movement forward, stumbling over his next few words. "The other night... there was—a—a friend was on duty, guarding the merchant. In his report the next day, he mentioned the Buk Toh had a few visitors. Nevilan was among them."

The world sucked in around Karadehti. Nevilan was visiting Taowen Isock? There was no way Nydera knew this or she would have said something. Had she not read the report? That wasn't a question for Nrus to answer. She needed to find out why Nevilan had visited the merchant.

"Who was the guard?"

Nrus looked disturbed. "His name is Tik. A good guy."

Karadehti was on her feet, straightening herself and dressing. "I want you to take me to him."

Nrus, still seated at her table as naked as his birth day, turned to watch her, glancing at his crotch. "Now?"

She answered more harshly than she intended, but this was urgent. "Yes, now. Let's go!"

"KARADEHTI TIASO," SHE ANNOUNCED THROUGH THE TENT FLAP when Tik asked who was visiting.

The tent flap was pulled back, and a man so tall he had to bend to peer outside filled the opening. Bare-chested, his brown nipples were at her eye level.

He took a step out into the sun, but Karadehti put a hand on his chest, halting him. He could have easily overpowered her, but a quick glance at Nrus, who gave a shake of his head, stopped him. Tik moved back into his tent, and she followed.

When Nrus stepped forward as if to join them, Karadehti turned, stopping him with a hand to his chest as she had done with Tik. "I need to speak with him. Thank you for what you've done." Her hand slipped down to his manhood. "I'll be sure to thank you more thoroughly later."

Nrus backed away, casting Tik a glance before Karadehti let the tent flap fall closed. She faced the man who was so tall his head almost rubbed the canvas roof of his tent.

"What can I do for you?" he said flatly. His voice was deep, like the rumble of the Sweet Waters River through its rapids.

"I'm worried about what happened at the prisoner's cage the last time you were on duty to watch him," Karadehti said, not wasting time. Too many things were going on, too many vulnerabilities, and not enough time to explore all of them.

"Nothing happened," Tik said, straightening his back. The movement made his long chest swell.

If he was trying to intimidate her, he would fail. No man, Freed or not, guard or warrior even, was capable of intimidating her. "I have it on good authority something did."

"Nrus?" the tall guard asked. His posture, his expression, gave away nothing. No displeasure, irritation, or humor.

Karadehti nodded.

"I can't think of anything that happened while I was on duty," Tik said flatly. "I apologize if this frustrates you, but it is the truth. Maybe you can help me understand what you're looking for."

"I was told Nevilan visited the prisoner."

"He did."

Aggravation tightened her chest. "What were they talking about?"

Tik gave her a one-shoulder shrug. "I don't know."

"You don't know?"

"No," Tik said, too quickly and full of confidence.

"How do you not know? Weren't you there?"

"I didn't listen."

"You didn't listen?" she said, hearing his agitation made her voice rise in pitch. "You would shame the Paramount by not doing your job?"

"My job is to guard the prisoner." Tik spoke as if he were describing a walk to the bathing pools. "I guarded the prisoner. Neither harmed or abused. My job is not to eavesdrop on conversations my superiors have with him."

"Nevilan is not a superior," Karadehti said with a snarl.

"He is Two-Marked."

This was getting her nowhere, a useless exercise that was wasting valuable time. This guard was either too imbecilic to answer or ignorant to genuine threats. Tall enough to converse with the heavens, and too dumb to listen to the gods' words. Karadehti had no more time to waste with him. "Was Nevilan alone?"

"No, the little one was with him," Tik said.

Karadehti spread her hands. "The little one?"

Tik was smart enough to register that gesture apparently, because he clarified. "The small one with the hook nose."

Rercan. Of course Rercan would have been with Nevilan.

"Thank you," Karadehti said, spinning and leaving the tent without another word.

She was outside Rercan's tent before her pulse slowed.

She didn't care what he was doing in his home or who he was doing it with. Grasping the tent flap, she flung it back.

Rercan was on his cot, reading a parchment. He bolted upright, whipping his feet over the cot and standing. In one movement, he tossed the parchment onto the bed, sliding to stand in front of it.

Karadehti crossed the short space between them, reaching behind and yanking her dagger freer. Steel against skin before he could open his mouth again. She pushed him back to the bed, straddling him once he was prone, the point digging and drawing blood.

"K—Kar—Karadehti, what are you doing?" Rercan said in a panic.

She lowered her face to his. She could smell the day's morning bread on his breath. "Something I should have done the last time I came here seeking answers. I don't take kindly to those who would lie to me."

"Lie? I have not lied to you, Karadehti," Rercan stumbled. "I would not lie to you."

"Yet you have not told me the truth. What does Nevilan want? What is he after," Karadehti said, pressing the blade deeper and moving it down the side of his neck toward his jugular.

Rercan whimpered. "Please. Please... don't. I will tell you whatever you want."

"That's the problem," Karadehti spat, continuing to draw the red line. "I don't want you to tell me what I want. I want the truth."

"I will! I will!"

Karadehti pulled the blade away. Rercan gasped for air, his eyes rolling back toward the head of his cot. But she was straddling him and had leverage. She pinned his arms down with her knees, almost straddling his face.

Rercan's eyes slid to her, widening. Whatever he thought she meant to do, he was wrong. Karadehti knew people thought she was so desperate to bear a child that she would bed anyone, even a Bound Boy, if she could find a way past the folded rings that imprisoned their cocks. Rercan almost smirked until she leaned sideways and placed the blade against the tip of his pinkie. She pressed the blade, and he screamed. With her free hand, Karadehti clamped his throat. She drew blood, feeling his arm flinch under her knee.

"When my hand leaves your throat, you will tell me the purpose of your visit to the merchant. Or you start losing fingers, and I won't stop until I've got the answers I seek." To prove her seriousness, Karadehti pushed until Rercan jerked, going rigid. She had cut deep enough for him to lose use of the tip of his pinkie. If he didn't start talking, she'd continue through to the bone.

She let go of his throat, and he gasped again before begging. "Please! Please! What do you want?" Tears leaked from the corners of his eyes.

"The truth," she said, putting more pressure on the dagger.

Rercan screamed. "We—he wanted to talk to the merchant. To find out what his story was. He wanted to know why the Paramount imprisoned the merchant. That is all. Please!"

"Why?"

"I don't kn—"

She pushed. "The truth!"

"I swear it! He wanted to know who the merchant was and why Nyd—the Paramount wanted him captured. I don't know anything more than that. He never tells me. I can ask. Please. Is that what you want? I will ask him and let you know what he says. I swear. Please give me a chance to prove myself."

She pulled the blade away but didn't move her legs to free his arms. Instead of killing Rercan to get the truth, maybe she could benefit more by being patient and giving him a chance to find out exactly what Nevilan was after. Greater plans were in motion and killing him now would only drive Nevilan to further secrecy. If Rercan feared for his life every moment of the day, she could leverage that and uncover Nevilan's plans.

Karadehti jumped to her feet, standing over the whimpering boy. "You will spy for me. You will report back to me nightly on Nevilan's actions and aims. If there is ever a threat to the Paramount, you will not wait until the sun sleeps. You will report to me immediately."

Holding his bloody hand, Rercan nodded. "I will. I will."

"Yes, you will. And if you don't, I will come back here and I will do what I did to your pinkie, to the rest of your body... as slowly as possible. Do you understand me?"

His eyes squeezed shut, holding his bloodied hand to his chin. "Yes. I do. I promise. I will spy on Nevilan and tell you everything I know. Please..."

"Go find the paladin for that finger before you lose it." She jumped to the thin rug, ignoring his whimpers, and stepped out into the open air, away from the iron smell of his wound. Tonight, she had made Olma-Ka safer for her sword sister.

11

NEVILAN

NEVER DID Nevilan expect his mission to be a simple one. Courage required not only risk, but luck and chance, and a good dose of patience. The reckless were not courageous. The courageous earned their reputation because they accomplished the difficult, and sometimes one of the most difficult things to do was to wait.

New suns came and went after his secret conversation with Taowen Isock, the captive merchant. Six of them. Just enough time to let the situation settle before he made his next move. Olma-Ka was in an uproar, worried about the attack on the guard, who was found at watch change at the new sun. Word spread about his slit throat, and before the breakfast meal was finished, everyone in the village knew the wide man had been nearly decapitated. Nevilan hadn't meant for such a gruesome death for the blubbering fool, but he couldn't stop Tocan once the man had started cutting. His bloodlust evident, powerful, undeniable. His Olmarian nature, true. Nevilan would remember that. They had meant to drag the body off into the desert, but Tocan's vicious attack had pushed Nevilan into shock, and he hadn't been thinking. He simply wanted away from the scene. Not until his adrenaline lowered did he recognize his mistake, and by then it was too late to go back.

Inquiries were made of Taowen Isock, but as far as Nevilan knew, the merchant hadn't given up their secret. Why would he? Betraying Nevilan as the culprit behind the guard's death only hurt his ability to break Taowen free. The merchant would remain quiet as long as he still saw hope.

Today, that hope sprang to life.

A few times each new moon cycle, Nydera would go into the field with the Freed women to train with the weapons and enhance her fighting skills. Today was that day.

The new sun barely woke when they had eaten and then loaded their weapons into a cart to drive out into the desert. Their training wouldn't bring them home again until just before the sun rested. Time was his friend today. Act, and deliver the mission.

All he had to do was get into the Paramount's tent. Thankfully, Tocan took care of a problem with that task as well. During the sun's last sleep, the faithful Bound Boy had dug a small hole under the back side of Nydera's tent. Without being caught, he covered it with a goatskin and a shallow layer of sand. Nevilan wouldn't need to interact with the tent guards. He would enter from the rear without notice once the way was clear, and leave the same way.

The Bound Boys and several Freed men were at the ditch project. The village's women were in the fields, crafting livery, sleeping or spreading on the Bed of Petals for any man they wanted. When the Paramount left with her Freed women for their training, the time to prove himself to Taowen had come.

As planned, he'd used his position to excuse Rercan and Tocan from their shovel work. Once in place, they started the planned argument as they reached the front of the Paramount's tent. What was nothing more than a supposed squabble at the meal in the Circle of Fire transformed into throwing punches. Nevilan had ordered them to be careful.

The intensity needed to progressively increase while not encouraging Nydera's guards to use force of their own to stop it. The men had to draw the attention of the guards as a distraction only. He couldn't risk his allies. There were so few. Now was not the time to put their lives on the line.

Staying on the periphery near the cellars, Nevilan watched. The hawkish Bound Boy threw back an insult as they neared the tent. Rercan reacted by pushing Tocan, who pushed back, throwing another heated comment. With a snap, Tocan put Rercan in a headlock and the two wrestled to the dirt, now just a short distance from Nydera's guards, who watched, smiling even as they shook their heads at the display.

Nevilan raced around the back side of the tent. Checking in both directions to ensure the way was clear, he felt around in the sand for the skin. Finding the edge, he tugged it away, exposing the hole.

He checked one more time before sliding underneath the flap.

Inside, he began his search while trying to ignore the thudding in his chest. On the far wall, he could hear the guards shouting encouragement to Rercan and Tocan to "break his face," and "kick him in the balls." The fight was entertaining them during yet another long, boring day that was just now only beginning.

This was working out better than he could have hoped.

Exquisite items filled Nydera's realm. The ruler of the Olmarians was living a good life, apparently needing little. In the side room, her ornate table, carved with a grand design of the rosewood forests supposedly representing the Hastelli Valley, stretched from one wall to the next. Twelve chairs surrounded the slab. Fruits filled large wooden bowls carved with designs from master hands. The bowls and table bore some of the finest craftsmanship Nevilan had ever seen. Separated by draped canvas into rooms, he began exploring the tent. In the second room, he found two chests of dark wood, highly polished, that sat atop hand-woven rugs of blue, a rare color in Olma-Ka. Rare, because it was expensive. Yet Nydera had somehow procured a ten-foot rug featuring the color. How many Olmarians could be housed in larger tents for the coin she spent on that rug? How much steel could have been bought for weapons for what she'd paid for it? In a third room, rich garments and a red silk robe hung along iron hooks latched on the door of an armoire as tall as he was. In each room where a thick pole supported the tent, weapons of glory—steel, onyx, the grandest weapons Nevilan had ever seen, stood silent sentry. Broadswords. Longswords. Shields as tall as a man, and bucklers as large as a bull's head, pronounced Olmarian battle glory.

Instead of a cot, Nydera slept on an actual bed. While the vast majority of people slept on cots, and a few still slept on beds of straw as they waited for the carpenters to build their cots, the Paramount enjoyed an actual bed. A bed!

Nevilan stepped to it, curious what one would feel like compared to his own hard cot, listening to the struggle outside the tent. The guards were no longer encouraging Rercan and Tocan to fight, now asking them to take it somewhere else.

Growing bored, he figured. He'd have to hurry.

He pushed the mattress with his fingertips. The mattress gave under his touch. He let his fingers dance along the foxfire blankets, enjoying their smooth, almost watery cool feel.

Lying on her bed, Nevilan stretched out, rubbing his hands on the blankets as he looked up at the roof, adorned with an assemblage of woven rivers of blue bordered in gold.

This was the good life. The aches, always a constant of desert life, were whisked away on the soft mattress, making it easy to ignore the scuffle outside, and the orders of the guards. This was a life he could live.

In time, though that time was regrettably not now.

To do that, he had to take the next step. Almost reluctantly, he swung his feet out of the bed. A sandaled foot caught the edge of the table at the foot of Nydera's bed. Most Olmarians were lucky to have a single table in their residence, but the Paramount had tables everywhere, each holding something expensive or unique. Sometimes both. This one held a smoking set. The water pipe had a broad, oval basin with a long stem projecting upward. A much thinner and shorter pipe jutted from the large bowl at the base. A thin membrane hose extended from the pipe, ending with a narrow, silver attachment. Small moonstones ringed it.

As it began to topple, Nevilan didn't have time to ponder the wealth in this tent any longer. He dove for the smoking pipe, catching it before it fell and placing it back on the table.

Off the bed, his pulse racing with the near-calamity, he refocused. The search began under the bed, then moved under the table next to it. He carefully opened cabinets and chests. None revealed Taowen's satchel. The tent was too large and filled with the riches of being the Paramount of Olma-Ka for this to be a straightforward task.

Or maybe the merchant was mistaken? Nevilan's heart still pounded.

Sweat beaded on his forehead, his back, his chest. His hands were slick. He had figured the satchel would be obvious, that Nydera would hang it prominently as a prize to be bragged about. A sign the rich merchant had been captured. A momento of Olmarian glory.

But Nydera had hidden it away, suggesting it held contents she wanted secured. More than a simple satchel.

Nevilan panted. Panic crept closer.

He stopped, forcing his body and mind to slow. Then he noticed the quiet outside the tent. Nydera's guards spoke in short, mumbled sentences. The fight had ended. His movements would be heard if he wasn't careful.

At the rear of the tent came a shuffling. Nevilan pulled the dagger from his belt and spun, moving as fast to the opening as was safe. It was his only way out of the tent, and now someone was prying around. They'd pay with their lives if it meant saving his.

But then a shaggy, dark-haired head popped through the opening. Rercan's pointed nose turned up, accompanied by a grin.

"What are you doing here?" Nevilan asked harshly.

Rercan scrambled into the tent. "I wanted to help."

Two could search faster than one, but they would also make twice the noise. Twice the chance for the guards to hear and investigate.

If they do hear us, Rercan can become the sacrifice.

Someone would have to take the blame so the other could deal with the merchant. Rercan was capable of only one of those roles. He could use the Bound Boy as the culprit, he as the protector of the Paramount's tent. A third Mark could come out of this if circumstances turned.

"I don't need help."

"Yes you do," Rercan said, moving closer. "There was an accident. At the training. A couple of the Freed were hurt. A cart toppled over or something. I'm not sure how bad the injuries are, but a runner came to tell the guards and ask after herbalists to tend to them. They're trying to find the paladin too. Soon, everyone will return. If I don't help, you will run out of time, and who knows when you'll get another chance to find it."

An accident? Injuries. Was it critical?

He slapped Rercan's arm. "Agreed. Help me."

The buzz of anxiety and excitement rose outside the tent almost as soon as they re-launched the search. At times, Nevilan wasn't even sure he breathed as he searched. With the clamor, they didn't have to be as quiet as his initial search. With each passing moment, the pressure to find the satchel squeezed Nevilan's chest. This had to happen. This time. If the injuries were severe, he wouldn't have another opportunity, not for a long time.

On the far side of the tent, Nevilan saw a swatch of brown. A sliver of leather poked out behind a chest he'd already searched. A table sat behind the chest, atop it, something he never thought he'd see unprotected and left out in all its traditional glory.

The ceremonial Freeing dagger.

Checking Rercan's location, seeing he was busily searching, Nevilan snatched the dagger. Lifting it, he examined the blade that had set him free.

Grinning, he tucked the blade into the pocket of his robe, ordering Rercan, "Help me move this." Nevilan pointed at the table.

They carefully lifted the table, shifting it sideways. Once it was out of the way, Nevilan bent, snagging the corner of the leather satchel and pulling it from its hiding spot. His long hair fell forward, and with an irritated flick of his hand, he whipped it back over his shoulder.

"Do you think that's it?" Rercan asked.

Nevilan freed the latch, flipping it open. The satchel was filled with coins, a bracelet, and more folded pieces of parchment than even the oldest elder in Olma-Ka possessed. "There's only one way of knowing, or chance delivering the wrong one to Taowen," Nevilan whispered. Pulling the pieces of parchment out, he laid them on the table and unrolled them, scanning their contents as he did. Rercan scanned alongside him.

"This one mentions Taowen. It's addressed to him," Rercan said, tapping the parchment.

"Good." Nevilan nodded, curling the pieces in front of him and gesturing for Rercan to do the same.

The satchel put back together, Nevilan's anxiety shifted to excitement. They moved toward escape. "You go first."

Rercan complied, falling to the tent floor and sliding into the hole and out of the tent in rapid twists of his torso.

Any suspicious citizens outside the tent would see Rercan and likely signal a warning, meaning the guards would vacate the front of the tent, leading to an alternate way out. The silence told him his friend hadn't been spied. Throwing the strap of the satchel over his head, Nevilan fell to the ground on his back, sliding under the flap and out of the Paramount's tent.

Outside, he got to his feet and brushed his robes clean. "Push the sand back into the hole. Let's get this covered up." Nevilan rolled the skin Tocan had covered the hole with and stuffed it inside his robe. The sand scratched his bare skin. He'd dump it near someone else's tent later.

Rercan was on his knees, filling the hole.

"Hurry," Nevilan kept watch while the Bound Boy smoothed and trampled the sand to disguise any evidence.

"What do we do now?" Rercan asked once they were away.

"We wait."

OPPRESSIVE DESERT DAYS WERE ALWAYS LONG, BUT THIS DAY passed with the lethargy of a giant slug. Throughout the afternoon, after the dinner, and even as evening fell, Nevilan fought the temptation to race to the merchant with the satchel. But the cloak of darkness was essential for their security. The operations could not be undertaken in the middle of the day, or even at dusk.

When darkness fell, he ordered Rercan to call on Tocan. As most of Olma-Ka slept, the three made their way to the merchant's cage.

"I brought this in case we need to keep secrets," Tocan

hissed, pulling his onyx dagger from his belt, flipping it in the air and catching the hilt with ease.

Nevilan shook his head. "No need for that. We have to be careful lest nosy women start asking questions."

Rercan cleared his throat.

"We should still be ready," Tocan said.

Nevilan stomped ahead. This was not a topic for discussion. "We exercise caution. Or didn't you notice how people are on-edge over the last guard you kept silent?"

Tocan sniffed, blinking rapidly.

Nevilan shook his head. "Let's go."

A different guard kept watch tonight. This one was a brute, but thick-brained. Nevilan knew Lestal from his childhood. They'd stopped talking sun cycles ago, when he'd learned just how dim the other man was. No utility in that friendship. So it had ended. Lestal was much more a warrior than the last, much fiercer in his appearance. His wisdom was proven yet again by discouraging Tocan. Were they to need to kill the man, the task would be challenging. At best. More likely, this brute would live to expose their actions. This called for charm and distraction, not force.

By the grace of the gods, Lestal seemed as uninterested in having a conversation with Nevilan as he did. Fierce in appearance, the guard focused on external threats.

The fool. All of them. The threat comes from within and they still look outside.

When Nevilan was Paramount, he would fill the warrior class with those who were not only great fighters but also distinguished thinkers. The greatest vulnerability of Olmarians was that they put too much focus on physical strength, and not nearly enough on mental vigor. It would be their downfall. The vulnerability of the comfortable. An avenue to his rise in equality. In power.

Taowen Isock watched them with the light eyes of a Buk

Toh as they circled to the far side of the cage. "How does the evening find you?"

"This has been a great day," Nevilan said, facing the imprisoned merchant.

"Has it now? For who?"

Nevilan nudged Rercan, who had the satchel hidden inside his garments. The Bound Boy discretely pulled it free, apologizing for sweating on the leather.

Nevilan took it by the strap, holding it so the prisoner could see it in the firelight. "For Olmarians and for you."

Taowen's eyes widened. Glancing over his shoulder at the guard, he tried to scramble to his feet, slipped and barely caught himself before he landed face–first in the sand. Trying to save grace, he stood more slowly, brushing himself off. "You found it."

"I did," Nevilan answered proudly, sticking the satchel through the bars while monitoring the guard. "I believe this belongs to you?"

Taowen snatched it, pulling it close to his stomach and opening it. He angled it so the firelight could light the contents. After a brief search, his head snapped up. "This is mine. You've done well."

"You mentioned this will help me free my people. It is not my place to search through your contents, but I had to confirm the satchel belonged to you. You understand, I'm sure. But that leaves me facing the mystery. What does that hold that will help us free ourselves?"

Taowen held up a finger, his blue eyes blazing with life that had dimmed before this visit. Holding the satchel at chest level, the merchant dug his hand inside. Though there was a nice collection of coins inside, so what? The letters? What could they possibly provide to a Sun Skinned in Hastelle? None of the contents were special enough to elevate Nevilan's status so he could challenge not only Nydera, but Olmarians' belief that they should only be ruled by a woman. Finally, the merchant pulled an arm ring from the satchel. It was the same one Nevilan had seen during his cursory search.

Taowen handed it through the cage bars. "Here. Take this. Keep it close. This is the key to your freedom."

Nevilan looked at the arm ring. Nothing was special about it at first glance. The band wouldn't fit many Olmarian arms, especially not most of the Freed men. A child's riches. The small ring was half the width of his wrist, so narrow only a youngster who hadn't hit puberty could slip it to the customary position of their biceps. This was not a warrior's band. It was bland, if he was being honest. The ring was gilded. Small slices had flaked off over the sun cycles. Possibly iron, Nevilan couldn't be sure. No jewels. No crafts-manship beyond the strength in the bend. Small inscriptions ran along the top and bottom edges in characters Nevilan couldn't read. To him, this was worthless junk. Had he plotted with an insane Buk Toh?

Nevilan tried to keep his expression as blank at this supposedly important item, the key to his rise. "How will this assist us?"

Taowen smiled. "That is a band of a secret society in Hastelle. It carries with it a message, unspoken, yet powerful. Showing that to the right people will earn you great favor and influence. In fact, I will give you a name. Show this man the band, and your freedom is ensured."

"What is this name?" Tocan asked, as if he had a role to play.

Nevilan kept his grumbling stuffed inside.

Taowen only answered to Nevilan. "You remember?"

"The name?"

"Yes."

Nevilan did. "Prosper Malnit."

The skin around Taowen's bulbous nose wrinkled. "He is the man you seek. Get to Hastelle and head to Merchant's Row. There will be a stall there, an elderly woman selling silk scarves. Show her this band. That will get you an audience with Prosper."

"Who is this man?" Nevilan asked. "Really?"

The merchant had already told him this Prosper could help. But how? Would he really risk a journey south across the open desert and into the Greenlands of the Buk Toh without knowing specifics? A madman's march.

Taowen turned away, dropped to his knees and dug in the dirt, out of sight of the guard. He looked over his shoulder at Nevilan. "He is the one who can set you free. All you have to do is show him that and help him find me. He will handle the rest."

Nevilan looked at the armband in his hand again, bouncing it. Solid, but light. To believe that this band would be the item that could change his fortunes was difficult to accept—a great risk to take. But leaders took opportunities when they came.

Watching the filthy merchant dig a hole to hide his satchel, Nevilan briefly questioned the sanity of this plan. What other options did he have, though? The Bound Boys, with few exceptions, were too frightened to act. They needed someone to be strong for them, to help them see what they couldn't.

He could be that visionary. He was that visionary.

But he needed help, and help came in this imprisoned merchant. Taowen Isock had no reason to mislead him. They were each other's greatest hope. Whoever this Prosper Malnit was, Nevilan was going to find him.

"How do you propose I get to Hastelle?" Nevilan asked.

Taowen, still digging, didn't look up. "That is not for me to figure out. If you truly want your freedom, you will act to ensure it."

12

GAERON

"Move this." Gaeron sneezed when Drulf helped him push the block from the pile and received a face full of dust as a reward. The block tumbled to the palace floor, where it rolled toward Chali. Chips the size of cooking pots broke as it fell, spraying forward.

The Chaos Bender didn't move as the heavy block of wall thundered past where she stood. She watched it go, returning her gaze to the two men who stood halfway up the collapsed wall and had sent the block tumbling at her. "Do you think you could make a little more noise? I don't think the Skinless know exactly where we are."

Fighting off another sneeze, Gaeron said, "I don't think they care about us anymore. Surely they've moved on by now."

Drulf stopped, straightened and wiped his sweaty head, which only turned the dust on his forehead to mud that spread through his short, blond hair. "Don't be so sure. What else do they have to do in this wasteland?"

Gaeron had no idea how many new suns had woken and gone back to rest while they had been inside the palace. The only measure of time was the depletion of their supplies.

They had enough tack for days still, but the water worried him. Even rationing it strictly wasn't helping. Soon, they would be without water at all, and that would spell their demise unless they found this gods-forsaken Crown of Spikes soon. Even if they tripped across it with the next block they moved, the race to find a water source was still going to be nervy. They had to figure a way to find a water source without heading to the Endless Oasis just north of the Borttel ruins, having to fight off a Skinless horde just for a drink.

"If we stay inside this palace for much longer, there won't be much of us left to snack on," Gaeron said, "Even you."

Drulf ran his hands down his chest, smearing more dust on his sweaty robe. He looked at the smear, tipped his head, and smiled. "After eating nothing but jerky and tack, I almost look like I have the flaw."

Chali sniffed.

Gaeron kept silent.

The flaw was a term reserved for Olmarian women, those deemed too unfit to be warriors. They were typically the smallest, thinnest women in the village. One thing he had learned over the last few cycles was that Olmarian women could be far more vicious than her men when ridiculing and ostracizing. If a woman was too skinny to be a warrior, she was too weak to bear children. At least, that's how the thinking went. If she couldn't have offspring, couldn't continue her line, she lost worth in the eyes of Olmarians. Having the flaw was not something Olmarians took lightly. To Freed women, it was not something joked about, and Drulf knew better. This was a result of their lack of nutrition and rest. Hopefully, it was the last mistake any of them would make, because the margin for mistakes evaporated like a shallow pool of water under the scalding sun.

"Sorry," Drulf said, noticing Chali's reaction.

She shook her head. "It doesn't bother me. I don't have the flaw."

She definitely didn't. Even after searching the Black Palace for days, finding no food, no fresh water, Chali somehow still looked glorious in her leather vest and short-pants, filthy as she was. She had kept her hair pulled up in the Warrior's Embrace, exposing her thin neck, still attractive even under a layer of grime and sweat. For Chali Danos, there were definitely no flaws, not in Gaeron's eyes, even if she didn't have all the curves many of the other Freed had.

Breaking his thoughts away from her and her sexy, slim throat, he reached behind another block, checking Chali's position once more before pulling it down and letting it tumble to the palace floor.

Chali shot him an irritated yet playful look.

He shrugged, smiling. "Sorry. We have to get this rubble cleared if we want to get through." When a sudden darkness passed over Chali's face, Gaeron jerked straight. "Is everything okay?"

Her head half-turned as if she was listening to something behind her. "Yes... it's nothing."

Was she being honest? Her reaction was so drastic compared to how lax they had become over the past days. He would have been happy to see a mouse or two, even a mischief of mice. Any sign of life would be welcomed. The silence of this dead palace had grown irritating. He longed to be outside this perpetual darkness, away from the smell of fat burning as they lit torches. Away from the smell of stale air and wet stone. Away from spider webs clinging to corners, and mysterious sounds too deep in the palace to pinpoint. As their water dwindled, each search took a greater and greater toll. Hopefully, the gods were kind enough to not expose them to a threat that required her and Drulf. Gaeron wasn't sure they would be able to cast more than feast tricks in a few days.

"Maybe we should try another room?"

"I feel like we've searched through all of them," Drulf said. "I mean, I know we haven't, but it sure feels like it."

"Agreed," Chali said. "I feel like we have explored the higher levels and the lower ones. But I can't be sure. How could anyone? This place is… well, just look at this chamber. It's vast. As large as any we've found. If the Desert King had a throne room, this could be it. Honestly, it's hard to tell with this collapsed wall hiding so much. We won't know until we move the rubble. Once you get out of the way, I can help. It'll be much faster."

Gaeron gripped another block about the size of his chest. Whipping his arm back, he slung it down the pile. "Not going to happen. You need to save your strength."

"Oh, I do?" Chali's tone held an element of danger.

"In case you need to save our asses."

"And what if we need you to do the saving?"

"I'm fine. Don't fight me on this… please."

From below him, the Chaos Bender grumbled something, then spoke louder. "Anyways, if I am correct, though, this might be our best chance."

"And if we find nothing?" Gaeron asked.

"Then we head back to Olma-Ka," Chali said.

"Empty-handed?"

Chali's eyes slid sideways, again going to whatever she thought she heard. When she answered, it was in a careful, quiet tone. "I would rather return home shamed but alive than not return at all. Climb down from there."

Her voice held a tension that unnerved Gaeron. He and Drulf shared a look before he dipped his head to the side, indicating they should follow the Chaos Bender's orders.

When he was on the floor again, he bent and picked up his battleax. Drulf grabbed his bag and weapon.

"What is it, Chali?" Gaeron asked, not sliding his weapon back into its holder.

She blinked rapidly. "Probably just my imagination. I

swear, I keep hearing things, but I can't pinpoint them. It sounds like it's coming from back there." She pointed toward the dark end of the chamber, where the light from their few torches couldn't reach.

Drulf stared. "Well, we haven't searched back there yet. Maybe we should? While we have energy."

Gaeron hefted his battleax. "I agree. If you're hearing something, and it may be coming from that direction, not from behind the wall of stone, I say we go. Anything has to be easier than moving that mountain." He waved a hand behind him, not even turning to look at the rubble that didn't seem to lessen as they moved it. He was tired of moving the heavy stones. His back aged twenty sun cycles already, he swore.

They each grabbed a torch and moved forward with cautious steps. Gaeron and Drulf spread apart in front of Chali. The orange torchlight flickered when a gust blew across the chamber. Drulf yelped, drawing scrutiny from Gaeron.

"What?" the big man said, his eyes wide. "Don't tell me you expected that. We haven't felt air move since we entered this cursed place."

"Afraid of wind now, are we? I can't wait to get back to Olma-Ka and tell—"

Chali's comment was so flat it stopped Gaeron in mid–sentence. "There is magic here."

They halted. No one adjusted their bags or weapons. Not even the wisp of a black stinger's wing or the scratching of an insect replied.

"I think the only magic the palace has is the power the darkness plays with our minds," Gaeron said. "We're hearing and seeing things where there is nothing. Now we're jumping not only at shadows, but at a cool breeze. The first fresh air I've smelled in... the gods know how long."

"Possibly," Chali said carefully, "but I feel a presence. It could be remnants of the Desert King's magic, but it could be something else. We need to be careful."

"So what do you say we do?" Drulf asked, scanning their surroundings, his shortsword held high.

"We keep moving... but with extreme caution," Chali said. "And if anything feels out of place, don't touch it until I have had a chance to examine it. If you hear something, hold your position and make sure all of us do as well. For all I know, we could walk into a magical trap. As tired as my mind is from being in here, I can't promise I'll break it. Plus, this place is strange. I feel... I don't know. Something."

"Well, now I feel confident." Drulf's laugh rippled with nerves.

"Then let's move," Gaeron said, leading the way.

The dark retreated as they stretched slowly across the vast room. No matter how large the Black Palace, dominating the landscape, Gaeron still struggled to understand how it contained such impressive chambers of stone.

The party had been throughout so much of the palace, searching every accessible area they came across. Many of the chambers were large. Yet none had been the size of this one. The entire Olka-Fa desert wasn't home to enough people to fill the space. What was its purpose? Gaeron bet people could have been born and died in this palace and not explored each of its reaches.

Gaeron hitched his stride and stopped, holding up a hand. Chali and Drulf skidded to a halt.

"What is it?" the Chaos Bender asked.

"I hear..." Gaeron focused on the faint sound. Then he recognized it, his mood lifting. He spun, not bothering to hide the smile on his face. "Water."

Chali and Drulf beamed.

"Water? Are you sure?" Chali absently rolled her lips in on themselves.

"It's close, but that is definitely the sound of water. Running water."

"What are we waiting for then?" Drulf said.

Gaeron agreed. His mouth salivated at the sound. He could almost taste it now. "This way."

Before long, a tall wall loomed over them, blocking their path.

"Are you sure this is the way?" Drulf said. "It still sounds like a trickle to me."

Gaeron put his ear against the cold stone. Water rippled from the other side, just quieter through the thick wall. "We're closer. Let's move along the wall and see if we can find an opening."

They did, pushing on, encouraged by the sound that never dissipated. Gaeron would wear out his ax blade cutting through this stone if it meant finding a fresh water source. As luck had it, he didn't have to. Feeling like they walked the length of the chamber again, the rippling became clear, no longer buffeted by the wall.

"I hear it now!" Drulf said.

"And so did all the spirits of the Olka-Fa," Chali chastised. "Keep your voice down."

Gaeron didn't like what her tone implied. The Chaos Bender was unsettled, and she wasn't fooling him. He never understood the arcane, and wouldn't trust it if it weren't for people like these two. It was mysterious, unknowable. But, just as he could wield an ax, spike, bow, or sword with his eyes closed, surely those who could tap into magic could see things he could not. Right now, finding the running water was his priority, but he'd be keeping an eye on her.

"Yes," he said as torchlight lit the no longer perfectly flat wall. A gold arch, shaped to resemble the wall's bricks, jutted out. An archway meant a passageway. Running water echoed clearly from the mouth of the arch.

"Come on." Gaeron pressed forward before either Chali or

Drulf could respond, rounding the corner, his battleax raised half the height of the torch.

"Careful." Chali said.

"Ion's beauty," Gaeron whispered excitedly as orange light danced around this new room.

A few strides inside, a trench as wide as a child was carved into the floor. Down its channel, black water ran from left to right. Gaeron kneeled, bringing the torch closer. The water wasn't black, but clear. Black stone lined the bottom of the trench, creating the illusion that the water itself was.

He cupped his hands and submerged them. The water was cold, possibly the coldest he had ever felt in his life. Pulling his hand up, he sniffed at it. No poisons. No taint. Not even mold. He swallowed his handful. Fresh, clean water. He cupped again and drank. And then again.

Chali was beside him, kneeling and dipping her water skin. "It might be quicker to fill your skin."

"Can't wait." Gaeron set the torch on the floor while cupping his hand and drinking while using his now-freed hand to fill his skin.

"I'm so thirsty." Drulf kneeled at Gaeron's other side. Not waiting for his skin to fill completely, Drulf pulled the skin to his lips, angled his head back, and emptied the contents.

The water skin fell from his hands and into the trench while his face remained skyward. The skin, nearly empty, floated down the channel toward the darkness at the other side of the room. Gaeron took a quick look at his friend, seeing that Drulf wasn't responding to his skin, and dove to save it before it disappeared under the slit in the far wall.

"What is wrong with you?" he asked, slamming the skin against the Buk Toh's chest.

Drulf didn't respond. Instead, he got to his feet, lifting his torch as far above him as his arm could extend, and pointed up with his free hand.

Chali scrambled to her feet. "By the gods."

Gaeron's gaze shot up, lifting his own torch to cast light higher. Hanging from four black chains angled in the corners of the room, was the Crown of Spikes. Had Drulf not dramatically filled his throat with water, they may have never seen the crown. Dimly lit by the crackling torches, the crown was as black as the Black Palace itself. A purple hue hovered over its edges, around its bends, barely perceptible. When Gaeron lowered his torch, the crown all but disappeared into the blackness above. Without Drulf's torch, it would have. He lifted his torch, now joined by Chali's, and saw the crown held a jeweled design.

"How do we get it?" Drulf asked.

Gaeron's eyes followed the chains holding it aloft. Each was anchored into a wall far above. Through eyelets, the chain was secured to the wall in hidden crevices, to the floor. Small cranks were set into the crevices. Gaeron slung his ax onto his back and moved to the nearest and grabbed the crank handle, forcing it forward. It was clunky, resisting his push. Spreading his stance, he put more force into the push. The mechanism shuddered. Deep within the wall, something cracked as Gaeron's unrelenting push forced it forward. Gears protested after ages of immobility. The chain slacked.

"Search the other one. See if you can move that crank," he said to Drulf.

The big man scurried to the other wall. "I found it. But... it... I can't move it."

Gaeron rotated the crank until the chain extended fully. He moved to Drulf, waiting for the Buk Toh to move out of the way, and then pushed against the crank. This one broke free just as the first had, with stiff resistance.

"Showoff," Chali said.

With the two chains loosened, the crown dipped, still suspended by the other two chains. Gaeron moved around the room, which was a moderate, oval antechamber. Setting the other two cranks loose, he worked them free and the crown lowered.

As the crown descended, Chali said, "Slowly. I don't want us to break it. I'm not risking that or losing any of those gems. The Paramount would have my hide."

As Gaeron cranked the last bit of resistance in the remaining crank, the Crown of Spikes descended within reach.

Drulf said, "I'll get it." He stepped across the narrow trench of flowing water.

A loud thudding reverberated from the room they had left.

Drulf stopped, one leg on each side of the trench. "What was that?"

Gaeron listened. "I don't know."

Low, under the trickle of the freshwater channel, something moved, either in the large chamber they'd cleared of rubble, or something much deeper in the palace. And much bigger. The water in the trench vibrated.

"Curses!" Chali said.

"What is it?" Gaeron asked.

"A defensive spell. I should have known! It was set on the crown. When Drulf crossed the water, it activated. Grab it. We've got to go. Now!"

Gaeron spun the crank, no longer worried about risking a few gems, and the chain fell to the floor, along with the crown. Drulf, still straddling the trench, caught the crown in a meaty fist.

"It's still connected to the chains," he said helplessly.

The rumble grew, as if a wall were collapsing.

Gaeron pulled his battleax and brought the blade down on the closest chain. It recoiled with a snap. He moved around to the other three, breaking each with a single swipe.

"These are going to get in the way," Drulf said, lifting the crown with the dangling bits of chain. "I might not have room in my bag."

"Just shove it in there," Chali snapped, checking over her shoulder. "We're in trouble. That's a powerful spell."

They moved toward the archway in a tight clump. The rumble was deafening.

"Go!" she shouted.

The pair raced back into the large room, toward the tunnel they had entered from ages ago.

Stone falling on stone thundered around the chamber, toward the collapsed wall that they had been working to clear.

Thud.

The floor shook under Gaeron's feet.

Thud.

Chali yelled as she stumbled.

Thud.

This wasn't a wall collapsing. The shaking was too rhythmic. A falling wall wouldn't tumble in equal time like this. No, this was more like Oltari's largest army marching. Just like...

Footsteps.

Out of the looming darkness and into the flickering torchlight, a rectangle of stone emerged, descending. Twice the height of Drulf, the rectangle was shaped from the same black stone of the palace's construct. The stone foot slammed down.

Chali mumbled as she conjured.

"Hurry, please," Drulf begged.

"Trying."

When moving the rubble on the back wall, they had lit half a dozen torches on that end of the room. Those torches were still lit, exposing a disturbing truth. The pile of rubble was gone. Where the wall they had worked to clear had looked like a mountain slide, there wasn't even a pebble.

"By the gods," Gaeron cursed.

"Is—is that from—from the," Drulf said, pointing.

"Yes." Chali's response sounded haunted.

The crumbled blocks had been removed by the defensive trap Drulf had inadvertently set off. The rubble they'd been clearing took on a new life.

Gaeron's head craned up at the gargantuan standing before them. A giant golem. Its head reached to the third floor of the chamber. The black palace stone forming this giant almost blurred into the background walls, except for its burning yellow eyes.

"You have stolen that which belongs to me," a deep voice boomed. The walls of the chamber vibrated with its cry.

The black golem lifted an enormous foot.

"Spread out!" Gaeron raced to the side.

The three split as the large stone foot raced toward the floor, pushing the air before it.

When stone met stone, the floor cracked. Gaeron stumbled. Somewhere, Chali cried out. Drulf did as well.

He scanned the room, looking for his two party members.

Chali was on her stomach and scrambling to her feet. The golem lifted the other foot to crush her, but she was up and sprinting away before it struck.

To its back, Gaeron raced forward, swinging his ax at the monstrosity's leg. His blade struck, sending sparks and chips of stone everywhere, but doing no actual damage.

The golem bellowed and slowly turned, stone cracking along its legs as it did.

"Keep it distracted!" Chali gave her instructions from somewhere behind the moving mountain that now faced Gaeron.

"Small human, I will crush you for invading my kingdom," the disembodied voice of the golem threatened.

"Help me, Drulf!" Gaeron shifted to his side as those large yellow eyes, as large as he was, stared down.

"How?" his friend shouted.

"Keep it split! Stay on its backside," Gaeron said, darting between the golem's spread legs to join Drulf on the backside of the giant stack of animated stone. "Hit it whenever you can!"

They swung at its legs. Chips and sparks flew. Gaeron struck for the tenth time before a fist half, the size of the bathing pool, slammed into the floor, widening the cracks it had already created.

The golem's roar rumbled through the large chamber as it straightened to its full height again. No chance of taking off its head.

If that's even possible.

Chali had retreated to the small antechamber to stand just beyond the archway, her back turned to the events in this larger room. From his vantage point, Gaeron could see her hands moving, but couldn't tell what she was doing. The golem's stone feet pounding on the floor drowned out everything else. Whatever spell she was working on undoubtedly would need to be the biggest she had ever cast if they had any hope of surviving.

He sprinted around a pillar, taunting the golem. "Here, you bastard! I'm right here!"

The golem stomped toward him, one gigantic step at a time. It moved at a tenth of the speed Gaeron could, but each of its strides covered fifty of his. That closed the distance in two strides. Drulf followed behind, swinging with his short-sword and chipping away at its legs.

Gaeron circled the pillar, the only thing separating him from the animated stone. As he did, he swung at the leg as Drulf attacked from behind. Stone flew, but the golem stood.

Gaeron raced around the pillar again when the golem tried to reach down with a humongous fist.

The giant roared. Surely, there was no way the minor damage they were doing to it was hurting it in any measure.

Still, he swung. Bloodlust fired his attempts, but not enough to sever limbs.

"We're not doing anything to it!" Drulf cried from its hind side.

"We're keeping it busy!" Gaeron said, racing behind the pillar as a giant foot broke the floor. His heart thumped, pushing more of the desire to break and destroy through him. His fingers throbbed.

The golem pulled back its arm, hand in a fist. Roaring, it threw its fist into the stone. A crack appeared at the top. Another punch and—

Too late.

The golem punched, and this time the top of the pillar shattered, sending thousands of pieces of black stone careening around the chamber, most of it tumbling straight down. Gaeron dodged the pieces by running backward into the rear of the large chamber.

The golem, however, did not give pursuit. Instead, it slowly turned on Drulf.

"Run!"

Drulf dashed toward the only remaining pillar. He wasn't nearly as quick as Gaeron, and the golem almost caught him.

"Chali?" Gaeron shouted, searching nearby for an effective weapon.

Gaeron lifted a slab of broken pillar wider than his chest. Hefting it, he moved toward the golem as it stalked his best friend. Close to his target, he screamed as he put all of his force into the throw. The slab slammed into its leg, collapsing its knee. The monstrosity fell to its knees, bellowing again.

Drulf scrambled along the wall. Gaeron raced to a second slab, this one larger than the first. Though he could lift more than any man he knew, this one required all his strength and focus. If this attack didn't immobilize the giant golem, he wouldn't have enough energy to do much more than avoid it until Chali's spell took it down. If her spell could defeat it.

Drulf was in the far corner, now with no place to hide, watching Gaeron with wide eyes. Sweat poured into his own eyes as he carried the broken pillar piece closer. The goliath was pushing itself back to its feet, but still not standing.

"Shit!" Gaeron growled as time dwindled. The shortest path to the monstrosity was attacking from its front. He didn't have time to attack from the rear. At the same time, the golem recognized the new threat.

"Die, human!" the deep voice boomed. It made another fist and began its next attack.

Gaeron was too far away and out of time. Drulf couldn't help. Still, he had to try.

With everything he had left in his core, he lifted the slab to balance it on his shoulder. If it killed him, he would destroy this thing's other knee. At least Drulf and Chali would get away.

With a loud cry, he pushed the broken slab off his shoulder, sending it arcing through the air. At first, he feared it would fall far short of the black beast. The fist was descending, and he was spent. Well within the golem's striking distance, well away from safety, doom sang its warrior's song.

The slab arced downward. Gaeron just hoped the gods were kind enough to let him see it before the golem crushed him under its fist.

The slab struck, pushing the golem's knee sideways, collapsing it. As its body rotated with the strike, its fist roared past Gaeron's head so close the gust it created threw him backward. The fist slammed into the floor instead.

"Look out!" Drulf yelled.

Dazed, the strike had not only thrown the golem off-balance, but combined with the momentum of its punch, had sent it spiraling. That much weight couldn't be stopped, and it crashed to the floor. The chamber shook. Overhead, something groaned. Dust fell from the heights. Gaeron's ears rang even as he flew face-first into the wall. He struck and collapsed to the floor. Blinding white light blurred his vision. His head split with pain.

He tried to roll over but felt bound, unable to tell up from down. Vomit rose in this throat, and he gagged as he spewed the bit of tack and water in his stomach. And he waited, blinded by the whiteness, for the golem to crush him.

Please tell me they got away, his thought came, slow. *Just let them get away.*

But the golem didn't crush him. Instead, a grinding filled the room. The golem roared, but was drowned out by this new sound, which was like a thousand wet stones grinding a new blade.

The white intensified. The grinding blared. Gaeron fell to the floor, covering his ears.

Then darkness and silence fell, replaced by the first flickering of torchlight and heavy breathing.

Hands under his arms pulled him up.

"Get up," Drulf said in a soft voice. "We've got to go."

Gaeron blinked to clear his eyes. Drulf came into focus, but the rest of the room was murky. Forcing his head up, Gaeron asked, "What happened?"

"Chali happened," Drulf said with an exhausted chuckle.

"Is she..."

"She's okay." Drulf gave a muted smile. "She's checking on the golem. Well, what's left of it. Good thing you weren't any closer or you'd look as bad as it does."

Drulf lumbered across the chamber with Gaeron's arm wrapped around his neck and his own around Gaeron's waist. By the time they were at the feet of the golem, Gaeron's vision had cleared. Chali was standing to the side of the massive pile of stones. No arms, head, or feet and hands to break with. If any of the blocks held those blazing eyes, Gaeron couldn't find it in this new rubble pile.

Cracking stone caught his attention. It didn't come from

the floor, or the remaining pillar, or any of the walls. The cracking came from what was left of the golem.

"You did this?" he asked.

The Chaos Bender's enticing lips spread. "I would have done it earlier if you'd gotten out of the way." She tipped her head at the rubble. "It's almost done, then we can get out of here and away from this blasted palace."

Fissures spread through the chunks, fist-sized pebbles, and boulders of blocks. Chali backed away, lowering her hands. Large rectangular blocks that had made up most of the golem broke apart, falling as individual blocks. Then those cracked and crumbled. Each time, the blocks broke into smaller and smaller pieces until they were the size of rocks. Even then, her spell tore at them from the inside, white light flashing in the fissures. In amazement, Gaeron watched as even the smaller pieces broke apart until the largest became nothing more than black dust.

Only then did Chali face them, her skin pale.

"You look like a Buk Toh," Gaeron said.

Her lips curled up. "You don't look so great yourself. But I'll give you a break since you're not only a Bonebreaker, but a golem breaker as well."

"Doesn't have the same ring," he said with a weak grin. "Plus, looks like you did the real breaking."

She punched him in the shoulder, doing more damage to her hand than him. "Let's go. I can't be sure that was the only spell the Desert King set to protect the crown."

They hobbled from the chamber, back through the rooms they had spent days searching.

"What did you do?" Drulf asked. "That was impressive."

"Not as impressive as you two thinking you could take on a golem all by yourselves."

"You told us to distract it," Gaeron said.

"I was waiting to see if you would decide to try to wrestle the thing, thinking it was a babite or something. Then I saw it kick your ass and figured I'd have to save you from your boneheaded decisions. That's the only reason I got involved. I was having fun trying to figure out how it was going to end."

"Thanks for waiting so long and giving me that chance to prove you right," Gaeron laughed.

"This way," Drulf said, supporting both and turning them toward a narrow passage, stopping only so they could each grab a torch.

Gaeron hoped Drulf was right. His shoulders burned. His back was tightening by the second. Exhaustion wracked his body. He could sleep. Right now, right here.

Too tired to see beyond the torchlight. Too tired to question Drulf's memory, which was far superior to his on his best days and Drulf's worst. Too tired to concern himself with anything more than being led to somewhere safer and warmer. Somewhere, the paladin felt comfortable stopping to heal them.

They reached the wall. Drulf grunted as he bent and helped them sit against it, holding up a parental finger. "Stay like that. Let me check if this is the door."

Gaeron allowed his back to chill against the cool black stone. He closed his eyes and fought off the sleep that would not be denied. Until they were safe, sleep would have to wait. Sounds and stale smells drifted into his barely conscious brain until he heard a loud click and Drulf yell. When he recognized the reaction was out of delight instead of fear or pain, Gaeron relaxed.

"Yes!" Drulf exclaimed. "And the way is clear!"

Light, blessed sunlight, streamed into the room, exposing a shower of dust.

Chali sneezed.

The tiny flecks tickled his nose, too.

Drulf pulled them fully upright and lowered his shoulders to allow them to wrap their arms around his shoulders again. He wore a goofy grin. "I never thought I'd be so happy to see the sun again. Well, at least the Dark Sands version of the sun."

"Nor I."

The short slide across the sloped palace exterior didn't help his aches, but those were forgotten when his feet touched the dead sands.

They covered a broad portion of the desert but were still within the confines of the Dark Sands. After days of seclusion within the chill of the Black Palace, shielded from the heat of the weakened sun, none of them were up for a full-out sprint home. Still, they put miles behind them, pushed on by the need to get to Olma-Ka and the desire to be away from the Black Palace.

"I hope to never see that place again," Drulf said at a later point.

Gaeron bobbed his head. Chali quirked her lips.

Thankfully, they had gained freedom early enough to mark the east and begin the long trek. They stayed true to the course through the night, navigating by the celestial suns, and through the next waking sun. The rests were always too short; the periods of walking in between them, too long. They looked worse for their experience, but as the palace faded on the horizon, the brown sands of home called.

"Should we make camp and try to get home tomorrow?" Drulf asked, kneeling in the sand, uncorking his water skin and drinking cautiously.

Gaeron was about to answer, but looked back toward the west, toward the center of the Dark Sands he hoped to never see again. Back toward the growing cloud that rose from the desert floor instead of descending from the permanent one that hung over this part of the world.

He was so tired, he couldn't groan.

That cloud meant one thing. Soon they would hear the rattling and clanking.

Gaeron patted Drulf on the shoulder. "Not unless you

want the Skinless as cot mates."

"Cot mates?" Drulf asked, recognition dawning on his face as soon as he spoke the word. He spun. "How?"

Chali pushed herself up from her bent position, her face still drained of color. "No one understands them that well to know how they sense us. Maybe it's because we tripped across that pit or left our scent all over their ruins. Maybe this is a remnant of the magic here? Another protective spell just in case someone escaped the golem. I can't be sure. The magic is too old. Beyond anything I understand."

Gaeron huffed. "The only thing we can be sure of is that none of us have the energy to fight them, and they will be on us before the sun sleeps. We need to get out of the Dark Sands and to the Sweet Waters. The river has to slow them. Right? Let's pray to the gods we can reach it before they catch us."

At times, they ran. At times, they walked. At times, it was a struggle to take another step. But with an army of animated dead pursuing, each of them found the motivation to constantly move forward. By the time the sun tucked just above the horizon, they had left the Dark Sands and entered the browns of home. The smell of water hung in the air. The Sweet Waters River was close. If they could reach it, they just might survive.

"I'm not sure I can continue," Drulf said, stumbling and falling.

Gaeron struggled to help him to his feet as much as he did to right himself. "Don't give up on me."

Drulf grunted, neither in agreement nor disagreement. His cheeks flushed as he almost fell again.

"Just make it to the Sweet Waters. That's all I want you to aim for. The Sweet Waters," Gaeron urged. "Let's see if those bastards can swim."

"I like that plan," Chali said. "They're skeletons. It's our best chance. Maybe our only one."

The tactic encouraged Drulf. They headed east, verbally

and physically picking each other up when they had to. Only Gaeron didn't fall.

From the west, the cloud grew, as did the figures on the horizon. First only dots of white, their details took shape as they pushed east. Their speed wiped any thoughts from Gaeron's mind. A blank skin now. No capacity for formulating a strategy or a way to defend three against a hundred or more. This was about reaction now, racing and pulling his party with him, carrying them when he had to.

Just when he thought they would be overrun, the rattling eased and faded the farther into the brown sands they pushed. The Skinless had stopped at the edge of the Dark Sands, long before the trio neared the Sweet Waters River.

"There," Chali pointed upriver. "That's where we forded last time."

"Let's go," Gaeron said, feeling new-found power in his muscles as the Skinless gave no sign of leaving the Black Sands.

"What are they doing?" Chali asked after a mile march northeast, toward the river. The skeleton horde had faded to blotches now.

"What are they afraid of?" Gaeron asked.

"I don't know." Drulf shrugged.

"Look at where they stopped," Chali said.

Then Gaeron understood. Stretched across the desert, the Skinless formed a single line as far as their ranks could reach. At the edge, where black met brown, where dead met half-dead, they hadn't taken another step forward.

He smiled. Then he laughed. Then he cackled with relief. Tonight, they would camp without fear. "The Dark Sands. They can't leave the Dark Sands."

Drulf slapped him on the back. "I don't know about the two of you, but I'm ready to make camp and eat every bit of tack I have left."

"Now that's a plan!" Chali said.

13

NYDERA

NYDERA SAW the way Olmarians glanced at the growing trench when they passed on their way to the planting fields. She saw their glances at each other when she provided updates during meals around the Circle of Fire. She saw the way some Bound Boys looked at her when she checked on the work details.

Her vision, she knew, was a betrayal of the old Olmarian way. To the people of Olma-Ka, she was scarring the land with the trench. What would they say when they saw the first poles set, buried deep into the desert and standing tall enough to block out the view of the open land? Their land. How heated would their protests become when they could no longer see the mountain range or the ridges of the Cliffs of the Morning Star? This was cowardice. To live behind walls like the Buk Toh. In too many minds, she was attempting to mutate minds to become docile. Just like the Walled Ones. The worst insult to Olmarians, and for it to originate with the Paramount cut the wound open each time it healed. But what choice did she have? Especially if Chali brought home the Crown of Spikes.

Nydera Alethero never considered herself a coward. She was the Paramount because she stood in the face of a failing ruler in Sariona Petrosiana, and defeated her in battle. Sariona had been the most feared Freed woman in Olma-Ka at the time, her authority unquestioned even as she led them down a dark path of selfish ambition. Needless raids on caravans. Forced battles with Scorpion Riders that netted no winners. Nydera had sworn to free the people of Olma-Ka, to set them on the right path again, to help them move forward as a people. She found a champion in Karadehti, her beloved sword sister. The woman took up the charge of converting some of Olma-Ka's frustrated ranks. Winning over the rest of the village was going to be a grander undertaking. A struggle she was still fighting.

The project was just the first step in ensuring the safety of the village for ages to come. Had Sariona been a Paramount first, a violence-seeker second, the project might not have been necessary. The previous Paramount's aggressive leadership antagonized enemies from near and far, changing the course of the village and its people. Her policies led to merchants traveling with what now constituted small armies. Her aggression toward Buk Toh strained relationships and led to the building of the Hastelli dam in the first place. There would be more defenses in the sun cycles ahead. There had to be. This was the new way of their people if they wanted to survive the generations.

Nydera couldn't do it without their support. She couldn't do it without their spirited labor. And she couldn't do it without all Olmarians pulling together in the same direction.

Who was she fooling, though? At some point, the truth would come out. Even with the support of everyone in the village, her plans to protect Olma-Ka needed more than her people. To finish this in time, before events turned against them, she needed coin for labor, wood, and materials. Lots of coin.

The fact made her lose sleep at night, feeling like the betrayer of her people. Already, rumors spread, carried on whispers around the fires after dinners during the long evenings while Olmarians passed time as the sun slept. Chatter started well before she had the Hastelli merchant, Taowen Isock, dragged into the village with only half the squad she'd sent into that foreign city. That incident had only exacerbated the poisonous undercurrents. The cost in blood had been great, the payout irrelevant to the people, not only those who lost wives or husbands, daughters or sons, but even those who hadn't. Those who lost sword sisters to Scorpion Riders were owed more than she was giving them. How did you ask a people to accept death, greater risk, future risk, while also asking them to turn away from that which defined them?

Was she breaking them? They wouldn't be the only ones. She felt like she was breaking apart from who she had been before rising to Paramount, losing the warrior spirit more each day.

Taowen Isock was breaking as well. The cage was tearing away the layers of his comfortable life. He was learning what it meant to be a desert person. And she had to break the merchant. But only to a degree. He was too valuable, too essential to their future. Once he saw there was no way forward but to agree to her terms to his freedom would he see the desert from outside the cage. He would work with her. He would work with the Olmarian people. The trade route he would set up would repay his debt and pay dividends to the village for the rest of their history. Even if he tried to betray them again, once trade began flowing into the village, he wouldn't be able to undo their progress. Never again would he rob from them what was theirs.

She had sent a warrior to retrieve the merchant. It was time to give him a taste of the freedom she had denied him for over a moon cycle. Now she needed to rebuild him, in the image of the Olmarian people he would spend the rest of his life serving.

Nydera heard the pair approach before Tik spoke.

"Paramount?" the guard said in his typical flat tone.

"Bring him forward," she said without turning around. She wanted Taowen to see her confidence. The merchant may have been powerful in Hastelle, but here, he'd be received at someone's back. An insult, especially from the Paramount.

The tall guard brought the merchant, his hands bound, to stand beside Nydera. "Should I take my leave?" Tik asked.

"Don't go too far, Tik. I won't keep him long," Nydera said.

"Yes, Paramount," Tik said and backed away.

The merchant had worn down significantly. Nydera wasn't surprised by his haggardness. The cage broke every-one. The only difference was the amount of time it took. The skin around his mouth hung looser. So did his rich clothes. Buk Toh clothes. Wool. Too hot for the desert. His white tunic was yellow with sweat and pulled open. The circles under his eyes were darker. The merchant was trying to hide the subtle sway in his stance. "Thank you for joining me."

"If I had a choice, I would have asked this long ago," the merchant said, dipping his head in deference. "I must say," he said, closing his eyes and sniffing deeply as he tilted his face skyward. "It feels good to taste the sun again. The cage you've kept me in provides so little."

"I imagine it does," Nydera said. "This doesn't have to be the last time you taste its heat. Repay your debt, and the sun is yours once again."

A moment of silence passed before he responded. "Repay my debt and you set me free?"

"Free to join us, to become part of Olma-Ka," Nydera said evenly. The merchant didn't have to like the conditions, simply abide by them. Better to have unfavorable conditions than death. She was saving him from that fate, and surely the merchant was smart enough to understand.

The old ways would not become the new.

"Paramount, you would humiliate me?" Taowen said, staring at the Bound Boys expanding the trench.

Nydera cursed Sariona's ghost for the crimes of her reign. Now it was down to Nydera to repair the relationships Sariona had ruined, and to leverage the others that would benefit Olma-Ka. Taowen Isock was part of the latter but had been one of the former. Olmarians did not tend to give second chances, but time was critical. Taowen would help her reach her objectives long before she could establish and fertilize relationships with other merchants. Her only other hope was a Sun Skinned merchant by the name of Hresh Utt. The man was from Ol-ta, but he hadn't traveled to Olma-Ka since Nydera had taken the title of Paramount. The road stretching between the villages had washed out because of Sariona's mismanagement. One more curse that gave her gray hairs.

"My people are not like the Walled Ones," Nydera started, her voice soft. "We live to be one with the land, harsh as it may be. Your people live behind their walls, inside their stone houses. Neither is more right than the other. We are different people. But that presents certain challenges to both of us. Mine is that I need to protect Olma-Ka. I need to defend their bodies while I change their hearts. This project," she said, waving in a smooth motion to the scene below. A long line of Olmarian Bound Boys pulled shovels-full of sand out of the trench in a constant blur of movement. "Is an unfortunate necessity. But it also presents challenges to my claim as Paramount."

"And you need it done as quickly as possible. To do that, you need the type of coin Olmarians don't trade in. Not usually. That is why you need me," Taowen concluded with too much levity for one in his position. "To force me into servitude."

Nydera stiffened, turning to face him and nod. Doing so

was more difficult than facing her enraged sword sister in a sparring session.

"A definite challenge, to be sure," Taowen said, "but not one I'm sure I can help with. My contacts and routes begin in Hastelle, not the desert. My entire logistical center is in Hastelle. To help in a manner you might need for this project and any future defenses, I would have to be there. Not here in Olma-Ka, where I have nothing. Something tells me, however, you're not likely to allow me to return to my home."

"I would assist you however I needed to, with whatever you would need," Nydera offered. "My people would do the same."

"That would still take time. Time I'm not sure you have at your disposal." Taowen drew a deep breath. "I know our earlier transactions were... unfortunately disrupted by my actions. I accept that. I will set things right with you and the people of Olma-Ka. But in terms of establishing a mercantile center here, I'm afraid I don't see that happening. Not in your time frame. I may never meet your expectations. There has to be another way, surely?"

"You're wrong about that," Nydera said, now squarely facing Taowen. "But you are correct about one thing. You will repay your debts and make things right with us. You will start by telling me what Nevilan wants with you."

The merchant, his short, fine Buk Toh hair disheveled, scrunched his dirt-stained face. An involuntary action, but one she caught and one he covered just as quickly. "Who is this Nevilan?"

"I think you know very well who he is. Let's not do this dance. Do you not think my own guards wouldn't report his actions to me? That he has come to see you numerous times? Do you take us for such a simple people? We are no fools, I can assure you. What is he after?"

Taowen bowed, spreading his hands. His temporary reaction of surprise was gone. This was a practiced politician, someone who depended on personality and charm, with decades of practice manipulating people and situations. "I'm afraid I can't answer that, Paramount. I have had visitors during my time in your cage. Sometimes," he said with a chuckle, "I confuse them for another. Your people look so similar to me. We could sit here all day under this hot sun and go through the list of Olmarians who have come, seeking to hear stories of Hastelle, the Shallow Sea, or even the Green Sea. Some have even claimed to think I know the secrets of the Lost Spirit Forest. Others have come for more insidious information. It seems half of your kind are disturbed by this." Taowen stopped and made a grand sweeping gesture at the trench.

Nydera's blood boiled. In her younger days, she would have throttled Taowen into the soft sand for such an antagonistic comment. As it was, she could not. They both knew that. She had not gone through all she had, had not sent a squad to Hastelle—ultimately to their deaths—to lose her temper and kill the man because he antagonized her. Even if her bloodlust was waking.

If Taowen wasn't yet ready to work with her, she would help him become ready. His existence was about to get much worse.

Without a word to the merchant, she turned away, walking back toward the village, and giving Tik a nod. "Take him back to the cage and make sure word passes that he is to not receive a meal today."

"Yes, Paramount," the tall guard with black curls that fell to his waist responded. Snagging Taowen by the elbow, he gave him a rough jerk.

She ground her teeth as Taowen laughed at her back.

They were still making gritty noises, as she threw open the flap of her sword sister's tent. "Are you ever dressed, sword sister?"

Karadehti faced away on her cot, exposing her nakedness

to the open flap as she straddled a man. Nydera couldn't tell who.

Karadehti looked over her shoulder, a flirtatious smile playing on her face, which was partially obscured by tendrils of curly black hair that stuck to her sweaty skin.

"Very few enjoyable things happen when one is clothed," Karadehti said, turning forward and continuing her gyrations on the man.

"I need to speak with you," Nydera said, allowing her chest to fill before she snapped at her best friend.

Karadehti's ass moved up and down, swirling in circles atop the man. "Can it not wait? I have not had my fill yet."

"I'm afraid not," Nydera said, moving to Karadehti's table, filling a goblet with mead, and collapsing in the chair. She drank until the goblet was turned upside down, empty, and then refilled it. "It's miserably hot today."

The man dressed, excusing himself profusely. Nydera ignored him. She had seen him around the village but wasn't sure of his name. He was thin in every place a woman didn't want thinness in a man. When he left, she gave Karadehti a quizzical look. "He's not one I would expect you to bed, sword sister. Are you running out of options?"

Karadehti used her palm to wipe sweat from her forehead. Her curls went with the sweat. She joined Nydera, naked, at the table, filling her own goblet. "I'm just exploring my options. A woman in my situation has to remain open to possibilities lest I never become a truly Freed woman."

"Fuck anyone who thinks that, Karadehti," Nydera said. "Nothing they say about you matters. You are every bit a Freed woman as anyone with children."

The joy from her romp vanished from Karadehti's eyes. "In your eyes, Nydera. But unfortunately, though you may be the Paramount, you don't form the opinion of everyone in Olma-Ka."

Nydera grumbled.

"Don't you agree?" Karadehti asked, tipping her goblet in Nydera's direction.

"Truer words may not have been spoken this moon cycle." Both women finished another goblet while she updated Karadehti on her conversation with the imprisoned merchant.

When she finished, Karadehti said, "Did you truly expect to sway the merchant? He won't work with us, Nydera. Maybe never."

Her bottom lip rolled over her top as she nodded in agreement. "We're going to have to make things incredibly uncomfortable for him. As frustrating as he is, I'm more bothered by the fact he mentioned numerous Olmarians going to see him. If half of what he says is true, he's been getting visitors the entire time. Even after I forbade it."

"Makes me wonder if we have a problem in the warrior ranks?"

Nydera fingered the goblet stem. "My fear as well."

Karadehti swatted her hand as if she were pushing away an annoying child. "We cannot know for sure that he was telling the truth. All of that could have been words to antagonize you, to distract you from the fact that he is developing plans himself. Taowen Isock is not to be trusted, sword sister."

"I know that."

"You know that, yet you're allowing his ploy to irritate you, at the least," Karadehti said. Her expression softened. "I'll work with the guards to deny anyone attempting to see him. Kill them if they refuse to comply. We could even move him into the village."

"And allow him to become comfortable? That won't happen."

"Then we double the guards. Triple them. Just don't allow this to skew your thinking. Stay true. Keep your focus on him and don't worry about what others are saying. Half of that probably isn't true. Even then, we will deal with those who might be plotting, in turn. You yourself have said that the merchant is the priority."

"He is."

Karadehti's palm flopped over on the table, rapping the wood with her knuckles. "There it is, then. Start making his life so miserable he regrets what he said this day. Forget the rest, for now. Well... except Nevilan. He needs to be dealt with as well, Nydera."

"Taowen denied knowing Nevilan," Nydera said, hating how weak her voice sounded in her own ears.

"He would," Karadehti said. "He is hiding something, protecting the bastard. We've both read the reports. Nothing more than a handful, mostly the boys who bring the meals, and too many gawkers interested in the foreign curiosity. Nevilan is different, and we both know that. We have to watch him. One time near the merchant is enough." Karadehti slapped the table with a flat palm, her dark eyes sparkling with deviousness. "The next time he steps near the cage, have the guards feed him the haft."

Nydera snickered at the popular saying. "I can't kill him."

"Wait, and you may never get the chance to make him regret his decisions."

"What do you propose? Besides killing."

Without hesitation, Karadehti said, "Kill him. In his sleep if you want to, though I wouldn't wait. Were I Paramount, I'd walk straight to his tent and slit his throat before our next meal."

"The old ways cannot become the new," Nydera said, shaking her head. "Plus, he better be working on the project, preferably with a shovel in his hands."

Karadehti smirked. "You and I both know that even if he was, the most work he's doing is holding that damn shovel. It probably has the cleanest head in the village."

"Not a scratch on it."

The women shared a laugh that faded as soon as Karadehti refilled their drinks. "While you think about what you'll do with Nevilan, you might find something else interesting.

"Oh?"

"I had an interesting conversation with Rercan. We may not need the merchant to tell us exactly what Nevilan seeks."

Nydera leaned forward.

"Let's just say I have encouraged him to spy and report back with anything of interest," Karadehti said, her face flinching. "I know the old ways are not supposed to become the new, but I did this for you."

Nydera's eyes widened, half thrilled by the revelation, half hesitant to give any sign she approved of it. "What did you do?"

Karadehti grimaced. "He may not have full use of one of his fingers," she said carefully, holding up her pinky. "But, had I not, he would have continued lying to me, perpetuating this game Nevilan is playing. At the cost of just a small piece of his smallest finger, he will spy on Nevilan."

She'd taken the tip of his finger? Nydera's anger flashed, not necessarily at Karadehti's actions, but at the need to do something like this in the first place. "And you think he will? Do you honestly think so? That he won't betray you to Nevilan, and now I'll have to watch your back in addition to watching him?"

"What will Nevilan do to me? I have nothing to fear from him. Plus, I did this for you so you wouldn't have to. Discipline me in public if you must. We will protect the truth together."

Karadehti could slay Nevilan in her sleep. But the oldest Andel boy was devious. His influence, growing. By taking the task, she'd also exposed her back for a dagger.

Nydera rubbed her face. Now she'd have to protect Karadehti as well. "The waters are lowering again," Nydera said, more to her goblet than her sword sister. She took a deep breath.

"Are we done discussing Nevilan?"

Nydera pursed her lips. "Not necessarily. I'm thinking the Bitter River might give us an opportunity."

Karadehti growled. "The Buk Toh have likely repaired their dam."

"We will have to send another party," Nydera said. "And this time they will need to destroy it completely. I misjudged the determination of the Hastelli to block the waters. We cannot make that same mistake."

Karadehti's eyes sparkled. "You're sending Nevilan?"

"Yes. And Rercan, along with Freed women."

Karadehti cocked her head. "That will take care of a couple problems at once. But you will need someone to watch Nevilan to make sure he does his duty away from your eyes. Someone who isn't intimidated by him. Someone who will guarantee he finally earns his Two-Marks. And someone who will ensure Nevilan does not return to Olma-Ka should he not earn them."

Nydera never looked away from her goblet as she nodded.

"You know I will do it."

Nydera simultaneously feared and hoped her sword sister would volunteer for the duty. She wasn't surprised Karadehti had done so eagerly. It was the right thing to do, but it was also the hardest thing to accept. Karadehti leaving Olma-Ka at this time—her one confidant—would create a void. Too large of a void. Not what she wanted, but what progress required.

"It is best," Nydera finally said.

Karadehti planted her elbows on the table, leaning forward. Her voice was firm but soft. "Nydera, look at me."

She waited until the Paramount, her sword sister, the leader the people of Olma-Ka needed to evolve them past their ancient ways, did. "This time, the job will be done right. Nevilan will no longer be a problem for you."

14

NEVILAN

OLMARIANS DID NOT HAVE a god of fortune, but something was smiling on Nevilan, if not the gods. Even now, after days of traveling, he couldn't believe his good luck. Having only recently worked out the agreement with the imprisoned merchant, Taowen Isock, he now had the simple arm band that would curry favor in Hastelle. His biggest challenge had been figuring out how he could get to the city of the Walled Ones to deliver the armband to Prosper Malnit. He had mulled over the possibilities endlessly. A conclusion about how to achieve that evaded him still. Then, by the grace of the gods, the bitch Paramount handed him the perfect solution. A chance to right all her wrongs against the bound men of Olma-Ka.

She selected him as part of a party to return to the Hastelli dam and break it so the waters of the Bitter River, which were lowering once more, could flow again. Rercan was also assigned. For days, Nevilan had to disguise his jubilation at the good fortune. Only when they were away from Olma-Ka, traveling in the small band, did he expose his joy.

Having traveled with Freed women before, Nevilan knew what to expect and when it would be safe to let his guard down. Even Olmarians couldn't be hypersensitive to their surroundings all the time, even their warriors. But he could. He was. That was his strength. Let them glamorize physical power. While they did, he was slowly chipping away at their base with his mental fortitude.

The journey to the southeast held safe crossings where the squad could afford not to move in a compact formation. It was healthier this way for all of them. Everyone needed space from time to time. Nevilan ensured he took his when the Freed women were distracted with their own thoughts of the coming battle.

The squad had spent the better portion of the past day separated, focusing on the mission ahead. Nevilan kept Rercan close while keeping everyone else away. They'd run through their plan over and over until they were both sick of talking about it. Both men were ready.

Rercan was unsure a day ago, worried about the feasibility of the plan, about the opportunity to execute, about intervention by accident or the gods. Maybe he secretly still was. But Rercan was weak, so Nevilan spent the better part of a morning providing a detailed explanation as many times as was necessary. The journey was boring, and this filled the time, no matter how aggravating it was to have to be so thorough. He needed someone to help him pull this off, and the thinner man was the only one he trusted to help him accomplish his task and set things right.

The waters of the Bitter River may be freed again when all was said and done, but that wasn't the end of this journey. What Nydera Alethero didn't realize when she forced him on this mission was that she handed him the chance to launch the next phase of his rise.

And her downfall.

Once again, they entered the small valley that sloped away toward the Bitter River. As they neared the river's valley, Nevilan remembered the last two times he was here.

Then, he'd been part of a small party sent only to find the cause of the lowering of the river water. That mission had turned into a battle with an ulteron, and the death of a Freed woman. The event that had provided him the opportunity to have his band broken and receive his first Mark. The beginning of the severing of his relationship with his own brother.

The second time he had come to the area was after the raid in Hastelle, where they had captured the merchant. Nevilan had killed the squad leader of a small band of Scorpion Riders who had torn apart the Olmarian ranks, earning his second Mark.

For this mission, Nevilan didn't care about earning another Mark. A far grander scheme was at play. Once it came to fruition, Marks would no longer be a factor.

Long before they approached the Bitter River, the band reformed. Nevilan was called to the vanguard even though his role was to support the warriors with his ranged arrows.

He turned to Rercan before leaving him farther back in the formation. "Remember what I said."

Rercan swallowed hard. "At the dam. I wait for your signal."

"Ensure everyone else does. Kill the first to deny the order." Nevilan searched his friend's eyes. The shorter man looked as frightened as a boy seeing his first breaking of the band and knowing he would have to be publicly humiliated one day in the same manner if he ever wanted to experience his own freedom. He put a reassuring hand on Rercan's shoulder. "This is a great risk. But with great risk, comes bountiful honor. We will be successful, Rercan. Do you trust me?"

"I... I do," Rercan said. He leaned forward. "I trust you. I'm just scared. This... if we do this... we can't turn back. We'll be—"

Nevilan's hand gripped Rercan's shoulder, squeezing. The smaller man stiffened. Nevilan brought his head closer until he and the Bound Boy were almost touching noses. "Do not say another word. This is the only way. This will happen, with or without you. But I promise, Rercan, should you fail to do your part, you will not see another new sun."

Nevilan shot his hand to Rercan's throat, pressing his thumb in the small indentation near the joint where collar bones met. Rercan's face scrunched, but the Bound Boy didn't move to break free of the hold.

Nevilan turned and strode toward his spot in the formation.

Not long after a pair of Freed women ran up and down the line, drawing the squad together again, the vanguard of Freed people dropped to the ground. Karadehti ordered them to crawl the crest of the cliff overlooking the dam. She included Nevilan in that order. He didn't object. From here, they had the perfect vantage point to survey the dam, so he could see what awaited. Plus, he'd have access to Karadehti's mind.

Five Freed women made up the smaller party. Nevilan was the only Freed man. Karadehti was the farthest forward. Were the gods kind, she would have been left back in Olma-Ka or died of dehydration crossing the desert. But Karadehti was a strong warrior. As the sword sister of the Paramount, she could cause serious problems for his plans, but Nevilan didn't let her presence dissuade him. During the trek across the desert, he had devised a way to deal with her if the opportunity presented itself. If everything went as planned, it would.

"Shit." Karadehti waved the Freed women and Nevilan forward. "It is mostly repaired."

"And guarded," Freha Olton, the ugliest Freed woman Nevilan had ever laid eyes on, said. Her pockmarked face did little to draw attention away from the fact that her dull eyes were drawn too close together. Ugly, but dangerous.

The Hastelli had done a lot of work on the dam in the time

since Nevilan last saw it. Whereas a party of four had been able to break it and free the river's waters moon cycles ago, now the dam stood at nearly its original height, but was twice as thick. The river still flowed over the damaged section of the wall, but it was a tenth as powerful as Nevilan remembered. A crew of Hastelli worked on the heights and at the base, channeling the river into an ever-narrowing course. But it was the Hastelli along the top of the dam, those not working to repair it, who caught Nevilan's eyes. Four archers stood on each side of the dam. On both the north and south side, a cluster of pikemen stood guard. Just downriver, an encampment stood along the banks, occupied by at least ten men who lounged, drank, and ate as they passed their idle time.

"I think we pissed them off," Karadehti laughed.

"Imagine how angry they'll be as we're ripping their chests open this time." Freha snarled.

"Let's crush them," Sammi Yulton, one of the Paramount's personal guards, said.

This was going to be dangerous, bordering on reckless, making it even more shocking that Nydera had included Karadehti. The Paramount never risked her personal guards for missions like these. Not only had she done so this time, but she also put her sword sister at risk. Simply to free the Bitter River. It almost demanded his skepticism. What was he missing?

Karadehti analyzed for a moment longer before responding. "We will need to be careful of their archers. They have the advantage atop that structure. Ours will have to keep them occupied so the rest of us can deal with the swordsmen and the pikemen." She detailed her thoughts for the ranged attack and how the rest would press the Buk Toh. She finished by saying, "We will split up, half the party heading down to the banks of the river to engage the Hastelli there. The other half will attack the small squad at the top of the dam."

"What about the squads on the south side of the river?" Nevilan asked, not impressed with Karadehti's plan. Today was not a day to die. He was too close.

"The Bound Boys will keep them busy with arrow volleys," she answered at once.

"That will be difficult. The river is too wide. It'll reduce our accuracy."

Karadehti rolled to her side. Sand covered her arm and spotted her leather vest. She narrowed her eyes. "That is not your worry, Nevilan. You will be with the force atop the dam. The Bound Boys only need to keep their archers on the south side busy. The rest of us will do the actual killing. Stop arguing and get in position."

The Freed women were up and moving. He hadn't planned on hand–to–hand combat. His participation was supposed to be limited to ranged attacks. Before he could propose an alternative, the squad was dispersing.

As Freha briefed the Bound Boys on their duties, Rercan shot Nevilan nervous glances. They weren't supposed to be separated, and the hook–nosed Bound Boy looked to be panicking.

Don't you dare.

The gods would have to be kind, helping Rercan to see how close they were so he didn't crumble or capitulate.

So close. I am so close.

Behind the cliff side, above and out of view of the Hastelli, they split. As one half raced down the banks, the half Nevilan was in sprinted toward the fight at the top of the dam. He dropped his bow, hoping it looked like an accident, and stopped to retrieve it to allow the rest of his half of the band to engage the enemy first.

The Freed women attacked with their typical ferocity, catching the Hastelli by surprise. Olmarians knew the desert, were part of it, and could navigate its sands on the sound of the wind. The Hastelli, and their steel plates, were as loud as a raging river when they moved. They were conditioned to that type of sound as a warning of a pending battle. With the Olmarian stealth, the Hastelli had been caught out and now scrambled to form a defensive line.

The Freed women jumped into battle, the screams of war sounding over the river, as Nevilan drew his arrow. Behind him, Rercan yelled commands to the Olmarian archers. A small volley of Olmarian arrows cut through the hazy blue sky. Two archers on the north side of the dam fell under the first volley, cutting their numbers by a third.

Nevilan waited for his open shot, glancing to the south side of the river and noticing the archers on that side moving closer to get within range. The camp's pikemen and swordsmen were racing for the bridge. Those guarding the south side were crossing the damaged section of wall.

He took aim on the pikemen in the lead and loosed his arrow. It missed the mark, striking a man behind him in the arm. It flung the man over the edge of the dam.

Both pikemen engaging the Freed women had fallen, but so had one of the Freed. At first, Nevilan couldn't tell how badly she was injured until a Hastelli kicked her out of his way to engage with another. The fallen Olmarian had lost her arm, bleeding out.

Rercan called again, and a volley was sent skyward, cutting down two swordsmen and an archer. Another volley flew, this time toward the banks of the river, where the other half of the Olmarian band engaged the defenders of the dam.

The workers, who had scrambled away from the fighting at the outset and were now being harassed by the Olmarians, were gathering a mishmash of tools to use as weapons.

Nevilan swiveled his bow in their direction. These men had no military acumen, racing haphazardly into the fray after ganging up on and felling a single warrior. He dropped one of them before nearly exhausting his quiver. The rest were soon lost in the swarm of fighting.

"Support them!" He pointed at the banks, not waiting to see if Rercan could follow the simple order. The sound of arrows cutting the air let him know he had.

The fierce Olmarian Freed finished the north side defenders and now moved forward to meet the pikemen from the south side. The narrow width of the bridge reduced the available strategies to both sides. With the Hastelli pikemen, the advantage was theirs unless the Olmarians somehow forded the river in time to outflank the Steelborn.

Death at the hands of the Hastelli would serve none of them. He hadn't come this far and risked what he did with Taowen to die at the end of one of their blades.

He turned his attention to the fading fight on the north side banks, shouting to Rercan, "Move the Bound Boys forward. Support the top of the dam. I'll take care of the rest of them."

Rercan shot him a meaningful glance. He then waved for the Bound Boy archers to join the top of the dam fight. After they moved into position, they sent volley after volley down on the Hastelli archers. Two Bound Boys fell, but more Hastelli did.

With both the Freed and Bound Boys atop the dam distracted, Nevilan could take careful aim on the rest of his targets. And he did.

Nocking, Nevilan took aim on any moving form and fired. Hastelli pikemen. Hastelli swordsmen. Hastelli workers. The archers helped, dropping the Buk Toh dead at the end of their shafts.

Stooping, he re-filled his quiver by stealing one that had belonged to a dead enemy.

Two Freed women were putting swords through the chests of the last Hastelli to ensure they were dead. With their backs turned, the women never saw Nevilan take aim. Never saw him loose his first arrow, taking one between her shoulder blades. The other, Nydera's own personal guard,

Sammi, spun. He almost laughed at how wide her eyes had grown. She held her sword high as she prepared to charge up the river bank. She didn't make it halfway before Nevilan loosed. It hit three feet behind her. He nocked another, fired, and missed.

The Freed woman neared the top of the bank. He fired again. This one fell in front of her.

Sammi was now sprinting toward the north side of the dam. Hatred burned in eyes that were locked on Nevilan. She opened her mouth to scream, and Nevilan loosed his arrow as he squeezed his eyes shut. He opened them again as the arrow punctured her throat, sending her flying backward in a spray of blood. He watched her twitch and die, the smell of her bowels releasing carried by the hot day's winds.

His heart thumped in his ears, deafening him to the sounds of the battle fading behind him. With no one alive on the north side of the river, he turned to face his future.

The battle had pushed south, as the Olmarians had taken out most of the Hastelli archers. The Freed women, with Karadehti in the lead, could only stand two abreast as they crossed the dam, pushing the Hastelli swordsmen back now that the pikemen had been eradicated.

A small cluster of Hastelli remained behind the two swordsmen, trying to hold off Karadehti and the other Freed.

Nevilan edged forward, allowing the battle to play out.

The archers continued releasing volleys at the exposed Hastelli. The Hastelli reserves died where they stood, leaving only the two Freed women and a pair of Hastelli swordsmen, who were now being pushed to the south edge of the river.

Nevilan was impressed. He knew the brave warriors his people were, but he underestimated how vicious Karadehti was. The woman moved with a speedy elegance far superior to even the most graceful fighter he had ever seen. His brother was likely Olma-Ka's greatest warrior, even at his young age, but even he didn't move like Karadehti. She was like a leaf on the wind. Had this entire battle taken place atop the dam wall, Karadehti could have defended the north side from invading Hastellis for an entire moon cycle.

She cut down one of the swordsmen when he fell for her feint. The remaining swordsmen turned and ran, rejoining the small group who waited at the base of the wall, spread out to avoid the Hastelli arrows.

The two Freed women attacked. The four Bound Boys moved as one with them.

"Rercan!" Nevilan shouted.

The Bound Boy pulled out of his sprint. His eyes widened. When he looked toward the south end of the river, he swallowed and nodded. It was time.

Nevilan moved behind him, and the two men raised their bows and took aim.

Two arrows flew south.

Two Bound Boys dropped into the river, Olmarian arrows protruding from their backs.

Another volley. Rercan's struck. Nevilan missed. The surviving Bound Boy spun, his mouth falling open. Before he moved to warn the Freed women, Rercan shot him in the stomach. He fell to his knees, his hands clasped over the blood spreading around his wound.

The Freed women felled another two Hastelli. Only three remained.

Nevilan pushed Rercan forward. "Now."

Both men took aim. Rercan loosed as Nevilan aimed at a Hastelli. The Bound Boy's arrow felled the Freed woman beside Karadehti. Nevilan took out a Hastelli swordsmen in the throat, even though he had been aiming for the center of the man's massive chest.

As Karadehti fought the last two Hastelli, she danced to avoid their strikes, deflecting their sword swings. Nevilan pushed Rercan forward again. They were within steps of the south side of the river. Bodies lay scattered on both sides of the water. Olmarian and Hastelli. More would join before the day was done.

One Hastelli, a thin man who looked like he hadn't grown the first hair on his balls, swung wildly at Karadehti, slashing her arm. A thin line of red appeared, small trails sliding down her brown skin. She yelled, leaping and spinning in the air. The move stunned the Hastelli, who backed away, his sword falling to his hip. It was a stupid mistake. One Karadehti took advantage of, slicing the man's throat open.

Rercan and Nevilan stepped off the dam wall and onto the sands. The southern sand of the Bitter River. They moved to the side to give Karadehti and the man she fought space to finish their battle. The Hastelli was a good swordsman, quick in his reactions, but he was Steelborn, bogged down by his armor. Karadehti's incessant thrusts and parries were wearing him out likely faster than the weight of his armor. She danced with her blade, always too quick for him to even start an attack. This fight would last only as long as he could defend himself. Karadehti was never under threat.

Nevilan raised his bow, drawing it back. His arm shook from the tension. Inhaling deeply, he calmed himself, controlling his breath. He held it. The arrow tip became his focus. Karadehti danced with the Hastelli, her onyx blade smacking against his steel. The sound of their individual skirmish filled his ears.

Destiny called. He loosed his arrow.

It spliced the desert air. The thunk as it sank into human flesh hearkened to him like a spirit's song. Onyx against steel halted. Ceased.

Rercan gasped.

The Hastelli man found Nevilan's eyes, his bottom lip jittered. He smiled at the Steelborn in return.

Karadehti, on her knees, reached over her shoulder with her now–freed hand. Her onyx blade lay on the sand. She tried to grasp the arrow, to pull it free, but it had invaded her deeply. Her hand grasped the shaft, but before she yanked it, before she could even give it a weak tug, she fell to the desert sands. Her body tumbled down the south bank of the river, toward the freed side of the waters.

"Please! Please!" The Hastelli man dropped his sword, begging.

"Rercan," Nevilan said simply.

A moment later, an arrow shaft protruded from the Hastelli man's face.

"It is done. The bitch will never ask you to spy for her again," Nevilan said, his voice hoarse. "Collect what you need, but be quick. We've got a long journey to Hastelle."

15

NEVILAN

EVEN A MILE DOWN RIVER, the orange light of the raging blaze lit a dome over the demolished bridge. Nevilan stood on the banks of the Bitter River, watching the dam burn.

"You're a fool for not checking all the bodies on the north side," he said. The comment was spoken to the darkness but aimed at Rercan, who was lying on his bedroll a few feet away.

The man didn't respond. Instead, his bug eyes stared up into the blinking suns in the night sky.

They were far enough away that the rage of the fire didn't reach them. The burning dam would draw anyone within forty miles who felt compelled to investigate. They had to get as far away as they could. Getting lost in the night and taking their chances with the creatures it hid. The camp was as far as they made it.

As far as he was aware, the dam was isolated. Populated only by dead Olmarians and Hastelli, Nevilan had felt comfortable setting it ablaze after he and Rercan spent the most of the day following the battle demolishing enough of it to start the fire. Afterward, it took half as long to wash the grease they'd used as an accelerant from their hands. The blaze would weaken it. The river it held back would collapse it soon.

"I'm sorry," Rercan said sleepily. "It took us so long to pull apart the dam, and I feared getting trapped on the north side. I wasn't thinking."

No, he hadn't been thinking. But Nevilan decided against chastising his friend further. To continue to do so now would defeat the message. He still needed Rercan. The man had his uses. Rercan had allied with him before anyone else. If the smaller man had to pay for any shortcomings, this was not it. That time, just as Nydera's time, just as his own time, would come. Until he was sure he could achieve his goals without the Bound Boy, he would exercise caution. Plus, he had seen the battles unfold above and below the dam. He had been responsible for the death of tenfold the number of Hastelli and Olmarian warriors Nevilan had killed. He had put an arrow through Sammi's throat and into Karadehti's back. Rercan was valuable to his short- and long-term plans.

Overthinking and worrying too much, Nevilan chastised himself.

"It's okay," Nevilan said kindly, turning away from the distant blazing remains of the dam and joining his traveling partner at their much smaller fire. "Today has taken its toll on me. I shouldn't abuse you or our friendship like that. Let's not discuss this further. Instead, we should drink this Hastelli wine in celebration. What do you say?"

Rercan sat up, smiling. "That would be great."

Nevilan reached down and uncorked the wineskin he stole from one of the dead Hastelli—one of the many items they had stolen from the dead. The operation had proven profitable, not only in terms of gear and coin, but the Hastelli wine was an unanticipated delight. Nevilan had pushed half a skin on Rercan during their journey west. He planned on enjoying a few sips while Rercan imbibed throughout the rest of the night.

They were too far away from the city to reach the forest. Another two new suns would pass before they could reasonably see the walls of Hastelle. Nothing and no one pushed them yet. The Bitter Rivers, newly freed, would reach Olma-Ka within the next new sun or two. Nydera would be pleased as she awaited the return of her sword sister and squad. She would know they were successful and would be waiting to receive her warriors. New suns would pass before she would begin to wonder why the squad hadn't returned. In that time, Nevilan would be in Hastelle. Safe. By the time Nydera sent a second squad to investigate the whereabouts of her sword sister and the small band of warriors, Nevilan would be beyond reach.

But tonight wasn't about planning the days to come or worrying about Nydera's response or things beyond his control. Tonight was about what was already accomplished and securing it.

A stiff wind swept along the Bitter River below. He held his shiver.

He passed the wineskin to Rercan. "Drink, my friend. Drink well."

Rercan did. Nevilan watched, enjoying the quiet of the night only solitude could bring. There were no settlements near. No towns. The trading road was miles to the east and north. The river buffered their backs. The trident was at least another day's ride, so he had no fears of accidental meetings with strangers or foes.

As Rercan drank, Nevilan immersed himself in the comfort he felt from the day's accomplishments. The Bitter River had become a personal token—a mark of his departure. Olma-Ka would never be the home it once was if he ever returned, which he fully intended to do. A different Andel would return to the village. How his fellow Olmarians received him was the great unknown.

Only he and Rercan could tell the tale of what happened this day, but he was no fool. Rercan was a Bound Boy. The Freed of the village wouldn't see him any differently. His word wouldn't hold any more meaning than it did now. He had left Bound, and he would return changed, in more ways than one. Nevilan knew what the people of Olma-Ka said behind his back when they thought he wasn't listening or his friends weren't near to report back. He knew how his brother felt about him. He knew how those who had seen him perform in the raid to abduct Taowen criticized how he fought the Scorpion Riders. In Nydera's eyes, he saw the truth of the Paramount's opinion. In all their eyes, he was Two-Marked because of happenstance and nothing more. His accomplishments, his kills, meant nothing to them. They were everything to him. When he returned to Olma-Ka, that would change.

The change had already begun. And it would continue tonight.

Rercan pulled the wineskin from his lips. "This is good. Has a pleasant taste of jasmineberry. Thank you for sharing."

"Do not thank me. This is a reward for what we've accomplished. We have done something great for our fellow Olmarians. We freed the Bitter River again. And since," he said, pointing back toward the dam, "we've fired that, the Hastelli won't be able to rebuild quickly. It will take them ages again. We're heroes, Rercan. Heroes! Unknown yet, but still heroes. One day, we'll be more."

Rercan hung his head.

"Why the reaction? Are you not proud?"

"I don't know if I can be. We've betrayed our own kind. Shittara will spite us for our actions."

Nevilan had expected this argument. "She will not judge us on this act alone. She is a wise god. She gave us the strength to survive her harsh lands. In order for us to lead our fellow Olmarians to a greater glory, this day had to happen. Ideally, I wouldn't have wanted there to be innocent victims. It is a shame, I agree. But we cannot forget that had we not, they would have stopped us. We would be the ones with the arrow shafts in our backs. All of Olma-Ka would have been lost. No, this was necessary."

"There had to be another way."

Nevilan pressed his lips inward out of frustration.

"We could have talked through it," Rercan continued. "I understand there were always going to be victims. But... there were so many. So many." When he looked up, his eyes were wet. Fear? Regret?

Regardless, a risk.

"It was necessary," Nevilan said. "Honestly, after all the time I've spent explaining it to you, I figured you would understand that by now."

"I understand it. I just don't think it had to be this way," Rercan said almost in apology. "We'll never be forgiven."

"There's nothing to forgive!"

"And when we get back to Olma-Ka? What will they say?"

Nevilan sat up straighter. "They will receive us as heroes because only you and I know what happened. When we return to Olma-Ka to free the merchant, we will also tell our truth of the day."

Rercan was shaking his head before Nevilan finished. "The Paramount won't believe us. Especially if we return with armed Steelborn who will free the merchant. That's cr—"

"The Paramount won't have a choice. Are you so blind as to not see that everything has changed? What we did today laid down a new mark for us. We can't go home as the people we were before, Rercan. I am doing this, we are doing this, to change how everyone in Olma-Ka is treated. For too long, a small group of elites have determined the course of Olmarians. No longer. Tell me, do you enjoy being bound?"

Rercan's head dropped again. "No. Of course not."

"Would you not like to enjoy a woman as a man should?"

In the far distance the low rumble of the burning dam partially collapsing answered for Rercan.

Nevilan lowered his volume, knowing now was not the time to berate. "And you are not alone. Every Bound Boy feels the same. Even the Freed men would like more of a say in how they live." He laughed bitterly. "Freed. None of us are free, not even someone like me. Two-Marked and as voiceless as a babe under Nydera's regime. We're still all prisoners to the whims of her and her elite council. That bitch Karadehti wasn't the only Freed woman who deserved an arrow. None of them were innocent. We did them a favor by handing out quick deaths. No, my friend, we don't have to worry about Nydera's thoughts when we return, because when we do, we will not be alone. We will change the path for all Olmarians for the first time in our history. We will make it a better path, a fairer one, one where men like us are seen for what we are, appreciated for who we are, never again to return to being bound."

Rercan gulped the wine. Their fire crackled into the night, slowly losing its heat. When the chill became too much, Nevilan stood and placed another bundle of branches on it. Rercan was in no condition to tend the flames, or stand for that matter. Small sparks swirled into the black night.

Pulling his dagger from its sheath, he adjusted the blackened chunks of wood with its tip.

He lost track of how long he stared into the dancing flames, moving burned chunks of wood around with his dagger, keeping the flames supplied with cool air. All the way up the handle, the warmth of the fire spread. Before long, the blade of the dagger glowed red, like the fire in his heart.

Rercan snored loudly on his bedroll.

Sitting with his arms wrapped around his legs, pulled up to his chest, Nevilan watched the other man, who had stood beside him for all of his adult life, and long before. The man who'd been there for him so many times, and knew so many of his secrets. A fellow plotter and schemer, even if he lacked the courage to see most of those plots through to their end. The Bound Boy was a weakling. An excellent archer who would make a wonderful ranger one day, if he was ever Freed. Rercan was an asset in many ways. Weak, but an asset. He could sneak into positions like a shadow. Everything he took aim at, he hit. But what his stealth and archery skills could do, his mind countered. Rercan could only see the moment he was living, never capable of entertaining what was possible in the moments, new suns, or moon cycles ahead. And he too easily cowed to pressure and authority. Returning to Olma-Ka with Rercan, a Bound Boy, was too great of a risk.

Nevilan stood, the blade of his dagger had lost its heated orange color but was still warm, holding the anger of the fire in its steel. Creeping to his sleeping friend, he kneeled beside him, leaned forward, and placed the tip of the blade against Rercan's forehead.

And then he carved out the lines of the symbol that would bind Rercan to him forever. Sitting back on his heels, he looked at the two bloody lines of the Mark, feeling neither regret nor excitement. How could he over something that had to be done, something that was necessary for the cause?

Nevilan slept well afterward as his friend, drunk on wine and a day's battle, bled. There was deep peace as he closed the greatest day of his life.

Greatest of many great days to come, he thought as he began to drift.

This day had not been an accident. Every step taken had been deliberate. Every action, successful.

Sleep came, heavy. Fulfilling.

HE WOKE TO SPLASHING. ROLLING OVER, NEVILAN LOOKED towards the rising waters of the Bitter River, a good three feet higher than it had been even last night.

Rercan kneeled in the water. With cupped hands, he splashed water on his face. His lips quivered.

"The Mark can't be washed away," Nevilan said as he stood and stretched, breathing in the fresh morning air. The most glorious morning air he'd ever smelled.

Rercan turned with caution, like a wraith was stalking him and he only noticed once it was upon him. His cheeks were pink from the dried blood he had been hurriedly cleaning. His fresh wound just below his hairline didn't have a chance to scab over, and Rercan's furious washing had busted it open again. Blood ran into his eyes. He tried to blink it away.

"Why?" Rercan cried in a wavering voice. "Why did you do this to me, Nevilan? You Marked me. I'm bound, and you Marked me! I can never go home now. They'll kill me when they see this!"

"Enough whimpering," Nevilan said, pulling the ceremonial dagger he stole from the Paramount's tent from its sheath and placing the blade in the hot ash. "I Marked you because I need you. I needed to make sure you would never betray me."

"I wouldn't have!"

Nevilan turned to face his hooked–nosed friend, shrugging. "And now you cannot. You need me and my protection. Without it, the Freed will tear you apart for the heresy of what you've committed. Women and men. Bound Boys have tried to Mark themselves before, and you know the penalty."

"Death by scorpion," Rercan said weakly, his hands dropping.

"Come here." Nevilan pulled the Freeing dagger from the

hot ash, wiping the blade on Rercan's discarded robe. He held it up for inspection until his friend joined him. The man's eyes, too close together, widened at the sight of the sacred blade. "But you won't be a Bound Boy after this day. Let's break that band. Then we'll get on the road to Hastelle. We have a lot of work to do."

16

GAERON

THE SKINLESS WAITED on the edge of where the black grains faded to browns and watched the eastward-bound humans. Gaeron watched them back until they fell out of eyesight. The animated skeletons never took a step out of their blackened kingdom, nor did they depart the boundary as long as Gaeron and his companions were in sight.

He couldn't relax, even when distance blurred them into a monolithic line of white.

The night had been a restless one, even with the river separating them from the undead, and the dark cloaking their location. The next night was better. Farther east toward Olma-Ka, they felt safe enough to build a campfire to stay warm. When he was honest with himself, Gaeron preferred the previous chilly night, because it gave him an excuse to get close to Chali. Even Drulf bundling against the Chaos Bender's other side, wrapping his thick arms around her and Gaeron, didn't ruin the experience. He still lay next to Chali and lived through the night to tell about it. Finally, a blessing from the gods. Tonight, however, he would be sleeping in his

After mead and meat.

When they handed the Crown of Spikes to the Paramount, she promised a feast night they'd remember until the stars fell. The way the village prepared, he didn't doubt her.

Nydera's cheeks shone like a mother's pride for their accomplishment. This woman, this leader, was true in her praise and joy. She had always told him she saw his promise, but now, as she held the spiked and bejeweled crown, he had tangible evidence of what he could do to earn her pride.

"It is exquisite," Nydera said, amazed. She lifted the crown higher, examining the jewels, grazing her thumb over a blue one. A topaz, he thought it was called. Even in the interior of her tent, without the benefit of the sun, the jewels sparkled. "The Crown of Spikes. The Desert King's crown." She set it on a pillow that Terron, a young Bound Boy, had brought. She fixed on the trio who sat at her table. "The three of you should be very proud of what you've done. You have changed the fortunes of the village." Her hand drifted to the black crown with its uneven spikes that replicated the mountain range it took its name from. Her touch was tender, as if she feared breaking it, "With this, we will be able to buy everything we need for the stockade. More, even." She laughed lightly. "The village may try, but we may never repay you for what you've done. Rest assured though, we will try."

"There is nothing you need to repay, Paramount," Gaeron said, embarrassed by her praise.

Even the wind seemed to stop rippling the folds of the Paramount's tent when Chali locked eyes with the Paramount and said, "They could be Freed."

Nydera raised her eyebrows. "Could they?"

"They have earned it."

"This is a great accomplishment, greater than most achieve in their entire lives, including many of the Freed. Had I known what waited in those dead sands, I would have never sent only three of you." Her finger danced along the crest of an angled spike. "But did they earn the Mark?"

Gaeron hated being spoken of as if he wasn't in the tent along with the Chaos Bender and Paramount. It reminded him of how Nevilan behaved. But having a say in this conversation was not his place. This was Chali's place to speak on their behalf. She was Freed, the leader of the mission.

He shared a look with Drulf, whose pale cheeks flushed. Gaeron focused on picking apart the pig leg on the gilded plate, a meal serving as the precursor to tonight's feast, provided by the Paramount as soon as the trio arrived. Though his eyes were on the strips of meat he pulled free, his ears were focused solely on the exchange between the two powerful women.

When Chali replied, her voice was strained. A red hue darkened the smooth skin of her neck, exposed by the ribbon of black hair she kept pulled up in the Warrior's Embrace. "They earned the Mark, Paramount, for what they went through. Multiple battles with the Skinless." She flicked her hand at Gaeron. "This one, I now call the Bonebreaker because he seems to love to smash the undead, thinking he can face a horde alone. He tried more than once. They also survived in the Dark Sands over most of a moon cycle. The fight against the golem alone earned them a Mark, nevermind the fact they are just as responsible for finding the Crown of Spikes as I am. Without them, you wouldn't have that in your possession now."

"All great accomplishments. I don't argue that," Nydera said with a head nod. "But did they earn a Mark? Have they earned the right to be Freed according to Olmarian customs?"

Gaeron glanced at Chali, whose nose flared as she tilted her chin. "I can attest to their actions and say that they have."

"Yet, you are not the Paramount and cannot make such a determination," Nydera said, not unkind, before drawing a deep breath. "This is truly an impressive accomplishment, but not one that can earn either of you a Mark. Change takes time. If I were to Free them, I will have stoked a slow-burning fire in the minds of those who already hold kindling. There are those who want to hold onto the old ways. Some of them lived under the old ways and still embrace them, no matter how I try to change their hearts. The time will come when a man doesn't have to kill a significant human enemy, a squad leader, an influential Buk Toh, a Steelborn, in a battle to earn his Mark, but that time isn't now. Unfortunately. Too many of our people are set in their ways, and if I were to Free the two of you, I'd have a rebellion on my hands. Sariona used to rule by the word of her decrees, rarely taking any counsel. I've lived under a Paramount who determines what is best for everyone by her mind alone. I've never been that type of ruler, and I don't plan on starting now. I'm sorry, but I cannot, no matter the significance of what you've accomplished."

"I know," Gaeron said, now shamed.

"Yes, Paramount, I am aware of that," Drulf mumbled.

Gaeron wished the conversation would move on or they would all engage in this meal so he could move on. This was humiliating. Whether or not his Buk Toh best friend felt the same, it didn't matter. They'd done their mission. They'd survived. In the moon cycles to come, the Paramount might send them on another mission where he could finally achieve his Mark and become Freed. Talk didn't free Bound Boys, so why bother? He had proven himself to the Paramount again. This victory would lead to more opportunities. He could ask for nothing more. He *would* ask for nothing more. Blood in the sand.

Nydera leaned forward, her eyes soft. "I feel for the two of you. If I could change our ways tomorrow, I would. It is already enough that I ask your brothers and sisters to accept the stockade project. It is not the Olmarian way, and some look at me as a coward." She paused and scoffed. "Many do, in fact."

"It is not cowardly," Chali said with a significant bit of heat in her voice.

"Many would disagree with you. The old ways cannot become the new. Were I confident it would be accepted, I would call the elders to the table and demand this change. We have talked about examining not only what makes someone Freed, but the value of placing bands on boys in the first place. They aren't supportive. Not all of them. Not yet. For now, I have to be cautious with the favors I ask of them. First, I need their support for the stockade, then I can work on getting support to change the Freeing."

"Yes, Paramount" Gaeron said before Chali could extend this awkward conversation further.

Chali huffed.

"Of course, Paramount," Drulf said, fingering the edge of his plate.

As soon as she finished eating, Nydera stood. The three stood along with her. They were being dismissed. The tense meal was finally over and Gaeron looked forward to eating and drinking until he passed out in a less formal setting. Sweet aromas were filtering through the tent already from the Circle of Fire. Within hours, he'd have goblets of mead to drown out the humiliation from this conversation the roasted pig hadn't wiped away.

"The village will eat well tonight in your honor. Prepare yourselves," Nydera smiled as she looked them up and down. "Maybe spend the afternoon in the bathing pool?"

Drulf chuckled. Gaeron cocked a half-smile. Chali simply dipped her head.

Gaeron asked, "Are we that bad?"

"The stables smell better," Nydera chuckled as she walked them out of her tent and into the sun.

"Then I will get on with that after I stop and see my brother. I'm sure he'll want to analyze everything I did wrong when I tell him of the Black Palace and Skinless."

"Not to mention the golem," Drulf added.

"Your brother is not here," Nydera said, her eyes flicking to the trio when they stopped to face her. "The Bitter River lowered. We think the Hastelli repaired their dam again. He was sent with a squad to investigate and free them once again."

Gaeron's cheeks flushed. "I'm sorry I failed you. We thought we had broken it. Maybe... maybe when the... when Meda died, I wasn't thinking clearly. I'm sorry, Paramount."

Nydera harrumphed. "You failed no one. If anyone failed, it was me. I did not send you with large enough of a contingent to completely destroy their blight on the Bitter River. We each can learn from our mistakes, and I learned from mine. This time, I sent a larger band. Karadehti led them. When you have time, maybe at the new sun after you've enjoyed tonight's feast, travel to the river. You'll see that the rivers have risen. They were successful. Your brother will be home soon enough to brag about his accomplishments instead of criticizing you for anything he may think you did wrong in the Dark Sands." She smirked. "Are you ready for that?"

Gaeron was not. He didn't want to see Nevilan anytime soon now that he learned his brother had yet another opportunity for glory. Another opportunity for a Mark. As if he wasn't insufferable as a Two–Marked. If the squad returned and Karadehti provided testimony to support a third Mark for Nevilan, Gaeron would have to move to the other side of Olma-Ka to avoid the indignation.

"Why the scowl?" Nydera asked.

Gaeron covered the slip. "My apologies, Paramount. I was just thinking."

"About what?"

"Nothing."

"Would you be rude to your Paramount as well as dishonest?" Nydera asked, her words sounding more like a statement, genuinely curious.

He felt his pulse quicken at the accusation. "I would not be dishonest, Paramount."

Both Chali and Drulf's eyes were on him. He shifted under their scrutiny. Most times, he could use force to change an uncomfortable situation, but this was the Paramount and two friends he respected more than any in Olma-Ka. This was diplomacy, not a physical struggle. An arena he'd never be champion of.

"Yet it visibly upset you when you learned Nevilan was sent away. Why is that?"

She deserved honesty, no matter how ugly. "He doesn't deserve it. Nevilan is a coward, but a coward with good fortune. Someone who has not spilled blood in the sand. To be Freed is a great honor. The greatest honor. To be Two–Marked? He deserves neither."

His words hung in the air. Nydera watched him without speaking. He felt Chali and Drulf hold their breath. But Nydera had demanded honesty, and he had delivered, as he always would for the Paramount. For Olma-Ka. Blood in the sand.

Nydera pressed her lips together. "The gods can often be cruel. Trust me, I hate it as much as you. Well, maybe not as much. He is your brother after all. But I have ideas that might be of—"

"Paramount!" a guard shouted as she ran toward the group. She pulled up, her eyes wide and blazing. Whipping her head to look behind her, she turned once more to the group and waved her arm to encourage them to follow as she shuffled back in the direction she'd come. "This way, please!"

"Nontoot, wait. What is—"

But Nontoot was now sprinting away.

The trio followed behind their leader. They ran past the

rows of tents, past the platform in the Circle of Fire where Gaeron had been humiliated by breaking the band for Nevilan, setting him free. Past the Bed of Petals where a woman was entertaining three older Freed men, dancing for them as naked as the day Aabiku created her. She stopped as the Paramount ran by, her arms dropping to her side. They ran to where the Hastelli trail led away from the village.

A wagon was turned sideways at the head of the trail, as if its driver wanted nothing more than to drop his delivery and race away. The driver was Buk Toh. Confused, Gaeron examined the pale-skinned man. No merchant. The foreigner was dressed in a colorful cloak that had to be too warm in the desert, maybe even too warm for Hastelle.

Nontoot stopped at the wagon, looking into its bed. She turned, the strain on her face causing deep creases. She backed away when the Paramount skidded to a halt. Gaeron glanced into the bed of the wagon, seeing a Freed woman who'd gone on the raid to Hastelle to abduct the merchant. He didn't know Freha well, but knew her as a respectable warrior.

"Freha?" Nydera said in a panic, reaching down to touch the woman's arm.

Freha Olton was ashen. Dark crescents formed under her eyes. Her lips were nearly as bloodless as Drulf's pale skin. Deep cracks split sections of them open. They held a sheen, like the driver had applied a balm to them.

Freha coughed into her blanket. Even in the heat, the foreigner had covered her.

"Found her three days ago by the Hastelle dam. Well, what used to be the Hastelle dam," the driver said, his accent strange. "Back then, she had enough strength to say a few sentences. Asked me to bring her to Olma-Ka. Said I would be paid. Been getting worse since. This road isn't easy to travel. Hasn't said much after that first day. Hasn't talked at all today."

Nydera only glanced at the man, nodding. "Yes, yes. You'll be paid. What happened to her?"

The man in the colorful cloak of reds, oranges, and yellows shrugged. "No idea. Just know the dam was destroyed. Saw the fires myself. That's what drew me in that direction the next morn. Entire thing was burned to the waters. Dozens dead. Thirty or so, I'd say. Was going to stay far away when I saw the wreckage. That's when I noticed the carrion birds circling and decided to have a closer look, in case someone needed help. Crows were a black cloud, I tell you. Too many crows. Knew it meant dead."

"Was there anyone else? Anyone alive?" Chali asked.

The man's eyes turned down, saddened to be the bearer of bad news. He scratched the white whiskers of his beard. "She was the only one. The others... the stench." He stopped himself, realizing how insensitive he was being. "Apologies. It's been a hard drive to get her here. Didn't think she would make it."

The dam was destroyed. Someone had burned it. That was why the Bitter Rivers flowed again. But the driver had said Freha was the only survivor. That meant...

Freha's coughing fit racked her body.

Nydera leaned closer. "Please rest, sister. You're home now. We will care for you."

She turned to Nontoot. "Get someone to help you set her tent. Find water and bread." The guard complied before the Paramount followed with another instruction. "Drulf, can you help?"

Drulf nodded and moved forward. The crowded Olmarians split apart to allow him to get to the injured woman. Gaeron watched as his friend placed his hands on the woman's chest. He closed his eyes and chanted quietly, rhythmically, so low Gaeron couldn't make out the words.

Freha's coughing fit slowly ebbed away. Drulf continued chanting, and her breathing slowed, eased, becoming less ragged. Within moments, her face flushed a healthier brown. Her eyes flickered and then opened with a sharp, but still weak, focus. They searched and found Nydera. Freha's voice was coarse. "Paramount."

Drulf backed away, his cheeks flushed. "She's stable for now. But she will need to be moved out of the sun and hydrated. She can rest for a bit, and then I will see to her again."

Nydera stepped to the wagon, grasping Freha's hand and holding it against her chest. "What happened? What can you tell me? Is everyone... where is everyone else?"

Freha shook her head, tears forming in the corners of her eyes, seeping down into her hair. Her lips trembled as she answered, "Dead, Paramount. They're all dead. We killed the Hastelli and freed the waters."

"We know. You've done well," Nydera said, patting Freha's hand, not relinquishing her hold on it. "They're all gone?"

"No. Not all." She stopped, her eyes trailing to Gaeron, locking on him. "Two survived because two betrayed us."

Nydera glanced his way as if he had the answers. With widened eyes, he shook his head.

The Paramount turned to Freha. "What are you talking about? Who betrayed us? How?"

Her cracked lips parted. "Nevilan."

Gaeron's stomach dropped as his rage boiled. "My brother betrayed you? How?"

Freha answered his question, her eyes slowly closing as she drifted toward sleep. "He thought I was dead, but I heard him. He ordered Rercan to help him kill everyone, Hastelli and Olmarian."

"No," Chali gasped beside him.

"Yes," Freha said. "He killed Sammi, Paramount. Shot her in the throat. Killed Karadehti, Paramount. I'm sorry! Nevilan killed Karadehti!"

Nydera looked like she was about to choke, jerking forward, her mouth gaping, but she did not make a sound.

"Where is he?" Gaeron growled.

Freha's tears thickened. "My shame is that I fell to my injuries. When I woke, he and Rercan were gone."

"You said they were all dead," Gaeron aimed his words at the driver. "Are you sure you did not see two men? One would look like me, but thinner, less muscle. Black and tan hair. Long. The other would have darker skin, a large, arched nose. Small man you could crush in your grip. Be honest, or I will kill you where you sit."

The man shook, his face changing as if he believed every word Gaeron said, and he regretted his decision to help. "I'm sure. I searched the area for a while." The man flushed, looking away. "I was searching... for anything of value. You understand. But... but, I promise, there were no other survivors besides her."

Nydera pressed Freha's hand to her chest, dropping her head. She shook. As if she were speaking to the ground, Nydera said, "Please, take her in your wagon to her tent. My people will direct you, and I assure your safety. I will reward you."

Drulf stepped to the driver's side. "I can show you where," he said softly.

As the wagon circled around the small group, its axle squeaking, and headed into the village to deliver the injured Freed woman, a dark silence fell over those who remained. Gaeron had no words for the Paramount, nothing of comfort to say. Now was not a time to comfort. Now was a time to break. To destroy. His rage blinded him to any gesture of kindness. All he wanted in that moment was to tear the world apart.

Nydera lifted her head, her eyes locking on Gaeron. "Do you still wish to become a Freed man?"

His throat, tight with heat, felt scratchy. "Yes."

Nydera watched him, her eyes flickering with pain before narrowing. "Good. Then I want you to find Rercan and Nevilan, and I want you to bring them home for the Paramount's justice. I will kill your brother."

He gave her a stiff nod. "Not if I do it first, Paramount."

THE END

TO FIND A BROTHER

Tasked by the Paramount, Gaeron must decide between
doing the unacceptable or the unthinkable.

Grab Battleborn, the finale of the trilogy.

REVIEWS HELP

If you enjoyed this book, I would really appreciate getting a review from you.

Reviews not only help other readers find something they might like, but they help me as an author. Your reviews are important to me because they allow me to see what readers like you enjoyed about the book and what I could have done better.

Thank you to each and every one of you who takes the time to leave a review!

NEVER MISS OUT!

Get the latest news, special deals, exclusive stories, first looks at book covers, and more by signing up for Paul Sating's newsletter!

Sign up for Paul's newsletter to follow all the news and special deals for upcoming novels, and to catch up on the latest regarding his podcast at http://www.paulsating.com.

EXCLUSIVE CONTENT EVERY WEEK!

More stories! Get exclusive Paul Sating fiction, including free audio books, in podcast form!

Get more stories each month by becoming a Patron! New exclusive fiction each month!

Become a Patron & enjoy more content!

ALSO BY PAUL SATING

FICTION

Epic Fantasy

Battleborn Books

Bloodborn (Free for newsletter subscribers)

Battleborn Trilogy

Fireborn

Rageborn

Battleborn (July 2022)

Bonebreaker Trilogy

King of Bones (Coming 2022)

War of Bones (Coming 2022)

Breaker of Bones (Coming 2022)

Crown of Thieves

Birth of a Thief (Free for newsletter subscribers)

Urban Fantasy

The Zodiac Series

(Same Story World As Rev Carver)

The Fall of Aries (Free for newsletter subscribers)

Bitter Aries

The Horn of Taurus

The Gemini Paradox

Cancer's Curse

The Pride of Leo

Virgo's Vigilantes

Libra's Liberation (Coming Soon)

Rev Carver Series

(Same Story World As Zodiac)

Angel Assassin (2022)

Angel's Creed (2022)

Horror

12 Deaths of Christmas

The Plant (Free for newsletter subscribers)

Suspense

RIP

Chasing the Demon

Nonfiction

Novel Idea to Podcast: How to Sell More Books Through Podcasting

Podcasts

Audio Fiction Podcast

(Free for Patreon supporters!)

Urban Fantasy Author Podcast

(Available on all major podcast apps)

ACKNOWLEDGMENTS

This bookThis book was a labor of fun. I just love books that takes us on adventures beyond the deeper character building stuff. Yes, I enjoy those as well—or I'd be in deep trouble, but sometimes

I just need adventures and monsters to fight.

Even though Rageborn is a Battleborn story, meaning there will be a good share of blood and guts, I enjoyed the writing of this book in a way that I hadn't in a long while. The biggest take-away from the Rageborn process came in the realization of how big I want to make this world. So, if the sales are encouraging, and the reviews back those up, I'll be exploring Oltari quite deeper in the future. This world has so many stories to tell.

Of course, I don't do this stuff alone.

Without my wife, Maddie, there's no telling what would happen with the voices in my head. I get these hair-brained ideas, and she's the poor sacrificial soul who has to hear all of them before they're fleshed out. You all don't know how lucky you are that she takes the brunt of my idea-purges. What truly makes her blood in the sand is that she doesn't even like this genre! Yet, she is always there. Always the first to walk the journey I take readers on. She's everything.

If nothing comes out of stories I tell, at least my daughters, Nikki and Alex, can see what it means to their father for him to finally live his dreams. My hope is that, with each book published, they see the art of the possible, and challenge themselves to grow and stretch, and work their asses off, to achieve what they want in life—just waaaaaaaay earlier than I did!

Scott McMillan is a local Olympia friend and the deepest pool of knowledge I've ever come across in life. Reading his Facebook posts is not good for my author career, because I could go down a plethora of enjoyable, upsetting, interesting, and horrifying rabbit holes. Thankfully, I can resist most of those pursuits, but he does catch me from time to time. He has an influence on the world of Oltari even I may not fully see yet!

Kevin Rowlands, because you've cared for years... and it will never be taken for granted!

To Paul's Peeps, the crew who get these books early and tell me what works and doesn't work with them. You continue to save my skin! A massive 'thanks!' to Louis Jackson, Natalie Aked, Kevin Rowlands, Allie R., Stephanie Mikkelsen, Erica Stensrud, Lori Peterson, Matt Guerin, Aubrey Hughes, Malcom Shotton, Drew Mannie, Audrey Bates, Luke Mayer, Montague, Mike Brannick, Cherie Davis, Darren Kalish, Steven Filson, Kailey Alessi, Audry Wichelns, Patty Root, and Nolan See!

Lastly, I want to thank you. If you're reading this, you've contributed to the success of the books and to my ability to spend time writing them, thinking about them, envisioning them, and trying to take them to places that will make them enjoyable adventures for people all around the world.

Thank you!

ABOUT THE AUTHOR

Paul Sating is an author, podcaster, and self-professed coolest dad on the planet, hailing from the Pacific Northwest of the United States. At the end of his military career, he decided to reconnect with his first love (that wouldn't get him in trouble with his wife) and once again picked up the pen. Years on, he has published eight novels and he hasn't even screwed up his podcasts, which have garnered over a million downloads.

When he's not working on stories, you can find him talking to himself in his backyard working on failed landscaping projects or hiking around the gorgeous Olympic Peninsula. He is married to the patient and wonderful, Madeline, and has two daughters—thus the reason for his follicle challenges.

Find out more about his other books and free podcasts from his website: paulsating.com.

CONTACT PAUL

How to Contact Paul Sating

Published by Paul Sating Productionsx
    P.O. Box 15166
    Tumwater, WA 98511
    paul@paulsating.com

Follow Paul:

- Facebook: www.facebook.com/authorpaulsating
- Bookbub: bookbub.com/paul-sating
- Goodreads: goodreads.com/author/show/16982359.Paul_Sating
- Instagram: @paulsating
- Pinterest: pinterest.com/paulsating
- Twitter: @paulsating

Printed in Great Britain
by Amazon

41851977R00131